"We haven't sealed our agreement," Brent said softly.

Marla closed her eyes helplessly as she felt his strong hands gently lift her chin. His breath was warm on her mouth just before his lips claimed hers. She pushed against his chest. She had to stop him before she gave in completely. The intoxicating musky scent of Brent's closeness, mingled with the sweet scent of cognac, was making her head spin.

"Still fighting me?" he whispered in amusement.

"I'll always fight you," she said. "Marriage will change nothing..."

Dear Reader:

We've had thousands of wonderful surprises at SECOND CHANCE AT LOVE since we launched the line in June 1981.

We knew we were going to have to work hard to bring you the six best romances we could each month. We knew we were working with a talented, caring group of authors. But we *didn't* know we were going to receive such a warm and generous response from readers. So the thousands of wonderful surprises are in the form of letters from readers like you who've been kind with your praise, constructive and helpful with your suggestions. We read each letter...and take it seriously.

It's been a thrill to ''meet'' our readers, to discover that the people who read SECOND CHANCE AT LOVE novels and write to us about them are so remarkable. Our romances can only get better and better as we learn more and more about you, the reader, and what you like to read.

So, I hope you will continue to enjoy SECOND CHANCE AT LOVE and, if you haven't written to us before, please feel free to do so. If you have written, keep in touch.

With every good wish,

Sincerely,

Carolyn Nichols

Carolyn Nichols
SECOND CHANCE AT LOVE
The Berkley/Jove Publishing Group
200 Madison Avenue
New York, New York 10016

P.S. Because your opinions *are* so important to us, I urge you to fill out and return the questionnaire in the back of this book.

Second Chance at Love™

BITTERSWEET REVENGE

KELLY ADAMS

SECOND CHANCE AT LOVE
BOOK

CHAPTER
One

MARLA STANFORD FELT her heart beat faster as she headed for Karl's office, but she wasn't sure if it was due to nostalgia or dread. She had adamantly refused to set foot in Quebec City for the last year, and now it was only her stepbrother's desperate plea that had managed to bring her back.

As she stepped from the elevator on the top floor, the painful memories she'd managed to block out ever since she had fled the city a year ago came crowding in on her. Marla closed her eyes, but a man's penetrating gaze and tender smile haunted her still. A shiver of apprehension ran down her spine.

She entered a brightly lit reception area, where Karl's secretary, Jean, welcomed her warmly. Jean took Marla's coat and left her in the outer office while she went in to see Karl. In earlier days, Jean would have sent Marla right in. Whatever was going on, it had to be important.

Marla looked around the room, noting that not much had changed in the past year. Her eyes caught her own

1

reflection in the mirror on the opposite wall. Her shoulder-length blonde hair was pulled back tightly at the nape of her neck, giving her a plain, businesslike appearance, and her large blue eyes, hidden behind glasses, were devoid of makeup. She wore a shapeless tweed suit that concealed her figure and made her look older than her twenty-four years.

Marla looked quickly away. Even she had to admit her clothes made her appear matronly rather than sophisticated. But she told herself she didn't care. Her intention was to discourage male attention, and in that she'd succeeded.

The door to Karl's office opened, interrupting Marla's reverie. "Come on in, Marla," Jean said. "He's ready to see you now."

Marla strode inside and abruptly halted in shock, her knees growing weak beneath her. She hardly noticed Karl standing nervously beside the door, because leaning casually against the desk, arms crossed, was Brent Stevens, his dark eyes piercing her coldly.

It had been a year since she'd seen him last, and his face was harder, harsher, more uncompromising than she'd remembered. His features did not relax as he surveyed her. Those cool gray eyes flicked over her impassively, and Marla cringed at his icy inspection. The warmth she had once known in him was gone.

He was as handsome as ever, she thought with numb detachment, and his expensive suit only accentuated the lean contours of his hard body. He straightened up and moved slowly toward her, and her first instinct was to bolt, to run from him and the powerful memories he was awakening in her.

Without thinking, she backed away as his eyes continued to bore into her. He hadn't said a word, but she could feel the tension between them. Although she was loathe to admit it, he frightened her.

"No," she cried in a hoarse whisper. "I don't want

to talk to you." Knowing only that she had to get away from his penetrating gaze, she flung open the door and hurried out of the office.

Ignoring the startled glances of the men and women at their desks, she ran through the outer offices and down the corridor to the stairwell. The door clanged shut behind her, and her high heels echoed as she raced down the metal steps. Then she heard the door shut again and the sound of a man's footsteps coming after her. She clutched the railing tighter as she ran, afraid she might fall. Brent was chasing her, and her only thought was to escape him.

She made it to the ground floor at last and braced herself against the door, grasping the doorknob, but it wouldn't turn in her hand. The door was locked! She was trapped. Frantically she looked around, hearing Brent's footsteps coming closer. Tears came to her eyes as she pounded futilely on the door. She spun around at the sound of his steps coming down the last flight and leaned against the door, panting, her eyes wide.

He stopped on the landing and looked down at her with amusement. Slowly her fright turned to embarrassment and indignation. Now that she was forced to meet him face-to-face, she wished she weren't at such a disadvantage. Resolutely she stood straighter as he descended the last stairs, his eyes never leaving her face.

He stopped when he was so close she hardly dared breathe. The corners of his eyes crinkled in cold amusement as he looked down at her.

"It seems I should have had Jean prepare you for my presence," he said. "You bolted from my office like a scared rabbit. Are you so afraid of me, Marla?"

She ignored the taunting tone of his voice and snapped, *"Your* office, Brent? I'd forgotten you were so possessive, but don't count on it ever being *your* office. If you and Karl are planning some kind of merger, you can forget it right now."

"You're very quick," he said softly. "And you seem to have recovered from your momentary panic. Or are you only pretending to be angry, Marla? You were always good at pretending."

She refused to answer, and he laughed grimly, reaching out to trace a line down her cheek with his finger, his touch sending tingling electricity all through her. He was staring at her, mesmerizing her with his eyes, as his finger trailed across her lips. "Or are you merely seasonal?" he asked in a low voice. "Is that it? Hot in summer and cold in winter?"

His implication brought color rushing to her cheeks, and he laughed again. She couldn't meet his eyes, knowing they were both remembering the hours they had spent in each other's arms, making languorous love.

"I don't want to talk about the past," she said quickly to hide her discomfort. "I just want to get this over with— whatever this plot is that you and Karl have hatched together—and get out of here."

"It's not that easy, Marla," he said quietly, and she swallowed.

"What do you mean?" she whispered.

"Let's talk about it in my office." His voice was silky as he took her arm. "Or my future office, if you prefer."

"It will never be your office," she hissed, trying to pull her arm away. But his grip tightened and she winced as he urged her forward.

"Come, my dear," he said. "I think the cold air here is souring your disposition." She gritted her teeth as he led her back up the stairs, never once loosening the relentless pressure on her arm.

She held her head high as they walked past the outer offices, and she tried to avoid the surreptitious glances directed at them. She had been so stupid to run from him like that. No doubt he was now secretly laughing at her.

Back in the office, Brent finally released her arm. She rubbed it gingerly and glared at Karl, who stood nervously licking his lips. "Marla," Karl finally pleaded, "we've never gotten along in the past, but this time you've got to help me. This isn't a trick. I'm really in trouble."

She opened her mouth to speak angrily, but Brent quietly asked Karl to wait in the outer office, and Marla's stepbrother fled with obvious relief. Brent closed the door firmly behind him, then turned to Marla.

"Sit down," he said, motioning her to a chair. "I'll get you a glass of brandy."

"I don't want any," she said stiffly, standing where she was.

He lifted one eyebrow. "Given your panic-stricken reaction when you saw me, I think you'd better have one. It might make what I have to say easier to take."

As he went to the bar against the wall, she wondered what he was going to tell her. He turned around with two glasses. "Sit down, Marla," he said. From the serious tone of his voice, she knew she had best comply. She would have to hear him out, it seemed.

Under his intent scrutiny, she obediently sipped the brandy, lowering her eyes as he came to stand in front of her, his arms crossed over his chest. Nervously she pushed up her glasses, then looked up in startled surprise as Brent reached out and took them off. "Since when have you started wearing glasses?" he demanded scornfully. He held them up to his eyes and laughed. "I see I was right. They're plain glass, quite useless. Why did you get them, Marla? To hide your lovely blue eyes?"

His voice was caustic, and she glared at him, refusing to speak.

Brent set his brandy glass on the desk and walked behind her. Marla turned toward him and mustered as much cool control as she could. "Give me back my glasses."

"Why? You don't need them." He held them deliberately out of her reach, then broke them neatly in half.

Marla gasped. "What did you do that for?"

"Because I don't want you wearing them again. Is that understood?"

As she stared at the broken halves in his hand, she felt stirrings of panic. What was he going to do to her next? It was ridiculous to feel afraid of him here in the office of her own company with so many people just outside the door. No ordinary man would dare intimidate her here. But Brent was no ordinary man.

She froze as she felt his hands on her head. He undid the pins slowly, letting her blonde hair tumble down around her shoulders. For a moment he let his hands linger there, and she closed her eyes, remembering other times when he had touched her.

He came to stand in front of her again and lifted her chin with one finger. She looked up at him, sucking her breath in sharply when she saw the cold desire in his face.

"Has it been just a year, Marla? It seems like an eternity." He leaned against the desk.

"What do you want, Brent?" she demanded. "Can't we forget what happened a year ago?"

He laughed without humor. "Forget that we were going to be married? I think you ask too much."

"Then can't we at least forget the bitterness between us?"

"Do you really expect me to just forgive and forget, my dear, after what you did to me? You were going to marry me. Then, out of the blue, you announced you'd only been playing a game."

Marla raised her glass to her lips with trembling fingers and drank to calm her nerves. When she looked at him again, she was more composed, and she deliberately made her voice cold with accusation. "Of course *you* weren't playing games, Brent. Can you seriously tell me you were in love with me?"

"You're a hell of a cynic, Marla," he said coldly.

"Now finish your brandy. I'm losing my patience."

"I'm getting tired of this myself," she muttered. "Just tell me what you want and let me leave." But under his piercing gaze she drained the last of the brandy.

"All right." He stood up. "I won't mince words, Marla. Karl thought he'd found a way to make a quick profit last year. He did some creative bookkeeping with the finances at Stanford Electronics and used the money for a personal investment." He threw her a dry look. "Needless to say, it was not a very ethical move."

"And the investment?" she asked, hardly daring to breathe.

Brent shook his head. "A total loss. Now Karl has to come up with the money in a hurry, or the company will fold."

"Damn him!" she cried. "I should have known he'd do something like this. How could he risk the company?"

"You know as well as I do what Karl is like. The company means nothing to him. To him it's only an endless source of money to be used for his own pursuits."

Marla nodded in resignation. It was true. She had been a fool not to keep a closer eye on Karl. All her life she'd fought with him over his deceptive personal and professional dealings.

"Am I to gather then that you're proposing to cover the funds?" she asked, her voice calm despite her inner turmoil. "You want to bury the company?"

"That's right."

There was the slightest pause. "And what are your conditions?"

"There are two conditions to my financial aid," he said. "First, let me make something clear. If I don't provide the money, Stanford Electronics closes its doors."

Marla narrowed her eyes calculatingly. "There are no other potential buyers?"

"None," he said bluntly. "Karl has not done a very

competent job of managing the company this last year. To be frank, it's not even a good investment simply at the price of covering the funds."

"But you'll pay the price," she said wryly, beginning to understand why he was doing this. Apparently, Brent's thirst for revenge was strong enough for him to make a risky business investment. It was worth it just to take her company away from her, the one thing he knew she loved.

"I'll pay the price," he stated flatly.

"And Karl and I must sell you our controlling shares?" she asked bitterly.

He nodded. "You can take all the time you want looking over the books and discussing this with Karl, of course."

"That won't be necessary," she said curtly, "I trust you." He raised one eyebrow, and she amended quickly, "You were never dishonest when it came to business." She tightened her hands on her brandy glass. "I don't see that I have any choice, Brent. I'll sell you my shares." She met his eyes bravely, hoping he wouldn't suspect the depth of her feelings. She felt absolutely devastated, as if her world had just been destroyed. Although she was numb with shock, a dull ache was already beginning to gnaw inside her. She stood up carefully, summoning a rigid control over her shaking hands.

But Brent stopped her. "Sit down, Marla," he said quietly. She looked at him quickly, then sank back down under his commanding gaze. "I told you I'd imposed two conditions on this transaction. I want you to understand that both conditions must be met before I bail out the company."

"And what is this second condition?" she almost whispered.

Brent took a cigarette from his pocket and tapped it on his palm before putting it to his mouth. He glanced at Marla, then cupped a match to the cigarette.

Marla frowned, feeling a warning tightening of her stomach. She remembered that Brent seldom smoked, reserving the few cigarettes he allowed himself for difficult business negotiations. She held her breath in painful anticipation. But still she was unprepared for his next words.

He exhaled toward the ceiling. "The second condition, Marla, is that you become my wife."

CHAPTER
Two

MARLA SAT ROOTED in the chair, too stunned to understand what he'd said. She had to be dreaming. This must be some kind of crazy nightmare.

"Would you like more brandy?" he asked in a quiet voice, but still she only stared at him. He took the glass from her nerveless fingers and carefully refilled it, then handed the brandy to her and walked over to the window. He stood looking out while she drank.

She watched his profile covertly over the rim of her glass. He stood with his arms crossed, his face betraying no emotion. The cigarette smoke curled lazily toward the ceiling, giving him the air of a man in total control, a man who would take what he wanted one way or another.

She'd always thought of him as strong, but now he appeared unmovable, his features hard as granite.

"You must be crazy," she murmured at last, half to herself. He turned from the window, and his dark eyes burned into her.

"Perhaps I am," he said grimly. "A man would have

11

to be crazy to marry a woman who once said she hated him."

She flushed vividly at the memory and quickly lowered her eyes to her glass.

"More brandy?" he asked politely, but she shook her head.

He crossed the room in slow, deliberate strides and crushed the cigarette out in the ashtray on the desk. He leaned casually against the desk and studied her. "Well?"

"You make it sound like you're conducting a business transaction," she said scornfully.

"I am," he responded quickly. "You've heard my two conditions, and now you'll have to decide if you'll accept them."

Her blue eyes glistened angrily up at him. "I think I made myself clear a year ago how I feel about marriage, especially to you."

"So you have, and very graphically," he said. "However, this isn't a romantic marriage proposal I'm offering you. This is a business arrangement."

"Why should you want to marry me now?" she insisted.

He paused, then shrugged. "As a man who must entertain a great deal I would find it to my advantage to have an attractive wife. And you're familiar with the company and its workings. You'd be a professional asset as well as a social one."

She flinched at his words. "You're being awfully cold-blooded about this."

"Did you expect anything else?" he retorted.

She laughed coldly as she met his gaze. "But why me? Surely you could find someone else to serve your purpose just as well."

"There are a lot of other attractive women," he acknowledged, "but you're the only one who's professed such intense hatred of me. Perhaps you're a challenge I can't resist. Or perhaps it's because you jilted me, my love. I'm used to getting my own way."

"So that's it," she hissed. "Your pride was wounded. And now you think you'll pay me back by forcing me into this so-called marriage. Well, it won't work. You can have the company, but I'm going back to Syracuse." She stood up and grabbed her purse, but as she started for the door she felt his fingers tighten on her shoulders, halting her.

"I'm not through with you yet," he said in a cold, uncompromising voice. He spun her around to face him, and she put her hand against his chest in an unconscious effort to keep some distance between them.

"I trust I've impressed upon you the seriousness of this predicament," he said coldly. His hands were still on her shoulders, holding her immobile.

"But I said I'd sell my shares," she protested, staring at his shirt to avoid his eyes.

"And I told you you had to agree to the marriage before I'd bail out your stepbrother." He forced her chin up, and she shrank back when she saw the iron determination in his expression.

"Surely you won't refuse to buy the company just because I won't marry you," she whispered, her shaky self-control vanishing in the face of his unsettling nearness. "That wouldn't be fair."

"Were you fair a year ago?" he demanded softly, and she closed her eyes so he wouldn't see her pain. *Yes,* she wanted to scream. Yes, she had been fair then, because he had never loved her. She had left him to save herself, and now he was demanding the impossible of her. "You'd ruin the company and my father's good name?" she asked hoarsely.

"That would be Karl's doing, not mine," he reminded her. "I'm only offering him—and you—a way out."

"A way out." She laughed hollowly. She dropped her hand from his chest, and immediately he drew her close against him. She felt unsteady from the brandy and from

Brent himself—the hardness of his lean body and the subtle masculine scent of his shirt.

He moved one hand to her hair to gently press her head against him, and she could feel the rhythmic beating of his heart beneath her cheek. He was leaving her no alternatives, and he knew that. She felt as though she had stumbled into quicksand. Although she desperately wanted to run, she could not. She was being inexorably trapped by a power stronger than she was.

"I can't," she cried as she forced herself to remember the year before and the way Brent had deceived her. She pushed away from him and felt his fingers tighten in her hair. Maybe if she made him angry enough he'd give up this insane idea and let her go. She deliberately made her eyes cold and scornful as she looked up at him. "I hate you," she said. "I'd never share your name or your bed."

She searched his face for a reaction to her words, and for just an instant she saw some unreadable emotion flicker in his eyes. Then his face became expressionless once again, and he stared down at her until she averted her eyes. But a firm hand caught her chin and lifted it again. There was only derision in his voice when he answered her. "You'll share my name only."

She was caught off guard, and he laughed when he saw the surprise on her face. "I have no desire to suffer your hatred in my bed, Marla. You'll sleep with me again one day, but when you do, it will be because you want it."

"You insufferable beast!" she cried, raising her hand to slap him. But he caught her wrist as she swung, his fingers locking around it in an iron grip that made her gasp. She tried to pull away, but he forcefully drew her hand to his lips and kissed it.

"You're a practical woman, Marla. You should realize the futility of your position." Still gripping her wrist, he led her to the door. "I've reserved the company suite for you tonight. Go check in and freshen up. I'll pick you up for dinner at seven and you can give me your answer then."

He opened the door without waiting for her reply, and she thought to herself how sure he must be that she wouldn't make a scene in front of the office personnel. They were all watching her out of the corners of their eyes, and she drew herself up straight and turned on her heel, jerking her hand away from Brent's grip as she left. She could hear his soft laughter and flushed angrily as she continued walking purposefully.

She saw Karl get up from a chair in the reception area, his rumpled tie and unkempt hair evidence of his nervousness. So now he and Brent would get together again and close up any loopholes they might have neglected. It was all so efficient and businesslike. And she was caught in the middle, between the company she loved and a loveless marriage with a man who would never be faithful to her. Damn! She had to think of some way out of this.

She hardly noticed as Jean brought her coat and helped her into it. "Thank you," she murmured in distraction as she started down the hall to the elevator.

Her fury grew as she drove to the hotel. So he thought he'd coerce her into marrying him with his threats and bullying. And then tell her it would be a marriage in name only! She gritted her teeth in frustration. No doubt he planned to keep company with his present mistress while Marla was kept busy giving parties and entertaining his business associates. Well, he had another think coming if he expected her to capitulate to him that easily. He wasn't going to have his way in this or anything else that concerned her.

She stalked into the hotel muttering under her breath. She'd show Brent Stevens a thing or two. So he thought he could waltz in and tell her she was going to marry him. She'd see about that.

When the bellboy had gone and she was alone in the

suite, Marla looked around dully. She hadn't been here in a year, but it was as elegant as ever. Quite befitting the future wife of the company's chief stockholder, she thought grimly. She threw her coat on the plush white velour couch as she walked past it, and then turned and came back, noticing for the first time the flowers on the glass coffee table—a small spray of violets. They were arranged in a simple glass bowl with a card attached. She lifted it with trembling fingers: *I hope these are still your favorites*. The message was cold and impersonal. But she didn't expect anything else from Brent. After all, he was conducting this crazy, unbelievable courtship like a business deal. That's all it meant to him.

She kicked off her shoes and padded across the rug to check the rest of the suite. There was a fully stocked bar behind the couch, an adjoining bedroom with a massive canopy bed, a bathroom, and, through the the door on the right, a sparse office with a desk. She frowned as she saw the half-open door of the bedroom. Cautiously she pushed the door wider and peered in. The bed was made, but there were magazines on the bedspread. Surely the maid hadn't been careless enough to ignore those when she cleaned up.

Her brows knitted in confusion, Marla walked over to the closet and opened the sliding door, then stepped back in shock. There were men's suits hanging there and two suitcases on the floor. Someone was still living in the room. She whirled around to place an angry call to the desk when a second thought occurred to her, and she went back to the closet. Bending down, she tipped one of the suitcases toward the light and read the engraved plate. Then furiously she slammed the suitcase back down and yanked the closet door shut. They were Brent's things! She might have known. So he had moved in with her already. She stalked to the living room and paced back and forth angrily. He was so confident of himself. Well, she was going to set him straight!

She stormed back to the bedroom and jerked open the closet door again. With angry energy she pulled out his suitcases, grabbed his suits and shirts off the hangers, and began stuffing them into the suitcases. The shoes and ties followed quickly. Marla pulled the suitcases closed, ties and sleeves poking out the sides, and dragged them through the living room and out into the hall. Satisfied with her work, she dusted off her hands briskly and went back into the suite, smiling to herself. Mr. Brent Stevens had just been evicted from her room. That would set him back on his heels.

She went back to the bedroom and set about unpacking her own things. She hadn't expected to be in Quebec long, and with any luck she wouldn't be, but she had thought to bring along two changes of clothes. She hung up the two dresses and smiled smugly, thinking of Brent's clothes in the hall. It was about time she took charge.

Then she sat down on the bed and picked up the phone to place a call. A minute later she was talking to Jack Phillips, her assistant in the Syracuse office.

"How are you, Marla?" he asked.

"I'm fine, Jack. It's good to hear your voice." She felt back on her own turf now.

"How was the trip?"

"Fine." She paused and drew in her breath. "Jack, there's a bit of a mess here in Quebec."

"I know."

"You know? But how? I just found out about it myself."

"I've suspected things weren't going well for some time. You know we haven't paid a dividend in three quarters."

"I know, but the business climate hasn't been good for anyone." She paused, then a note of suspicion crept into her voice. "Did Karl try to get money from you, Jack?"

"No, no. It wasn't Karl. Marla, I received a special

delivery letter from Brent Stevens today. He detailed all of the company's financial problems."

"He did?" Her voice was weak with shock. "How does it look, Jack?"

"Not good. Mr. Stevens didn't give me all the details about what Karl's been doing, but frankly I don't see any way out for the company."

"Did he tell you he's offered to buy controlling shares?"

"Yes."

"And?"

"I think you'll have to sell, Marla. From what I've seen there's no other way out."

She closed her eyes, feeling as though a noose were tightening around her neck. "That's not all, Jack." She swallowed hard. "Brent won't buy the shares unless I agree to marry him."

There was silence on the other end, and then Jack said, "That's something you'll have to decide for yourself, Marla."

"But I need help, Jack. I don't want to marry Brent."

"Maybe you shouldn't be telling me this, Marla. It seems to me it's between you and Mr. Stevens."

"But you've been a good friend to me. I trust you to tell me the truth. Isn't there some other way out? Can't we raise the money somehow?"

"I wish I could help you, Marla, but no one else is going to have enough cash right now to buy the shares. We need it fast, real fast, or we're going under." He paused and sighed heavily. "Marla, I know this isn't any of my business—and you've never talked about it—but you were engaged to marry Mr. Stevens a year ago."

"Things changed," she said quickly. "Are you sure there's nothing else we can do?"

"I'm sorry, Marla. I wish I could be more helpful. It seems Karl has really done it this time."

"Yes, it does," she said softly, feeling her last hope

slip away. "Jack, will you take over the office there until I get things straightened out here?"

"Sure, Marla, whatever you say."

"Thanks. I'll talk to you soon." She hung up and sat staring at the wall, her pulse racing. So she would have to sell her shares to Brent after all. Well, she was prepared to do that. But would he let it go at that? She chewed her lip nervously. He had said she'd have to meet both of his conditions, and if she knew Brent, he would insist on that. She would have to marry him or see the company ruined.

She lay down on the bed and pounded the pillow with her fist. Damn him. He was giving her no way out. He'd even sent Jack the financial picture, just to make sure she had no allies.

There was no way Jack could help her. He was her best friend, practically her only friend, and like a brother to her. For the last year she'd determinedly avoided getting close to anyone, revealing little of herself. She and Jack had worked together and shared the burden of running the Syracuse office, yet even he didn't know her very well. She hadn't let anyone close to her since Brent. She was determined not to be hurt again, not by anyone.

Marla curled up on the bed, her fists clenched against her chin. She was so tired, so shaken by the encounter with Brent. If she could just take a short nap. Then she remembered that all she'd brought were the two dresses. She sat up and slipped off the tweed suit, then laid it carefully over a chair, and got the extra blanket from the shelf in the closet. She'd just take a short rest on the bed. She wouldn't even have to disturb the sheets, and then she'd be ready to face Brent again.

She curled up again in her slip and pulled up the blanket, snuggling down into its warmth.

Her fitful sleep was invaded by dreams of her stepfather, his laughing face looming before her. She was a little girl in Quebec, back in her own bed, her slumber broken by the frequent loud arguments of her mother and stepfather, Mason. Each fight seemed louder than the one before.

Sometimes she'd go off to a corner by herself and cry, hating to see the misery in her mother's eyes. If her stepbrother, Karl, found her, he'd tease her mercilessly until her misery turned to fury, and she would attack him like a spitfire.

Every night the living nightmare would begin again. On one particular night Marla was awakened from a deep sleep by the sound of shouting in the next room. Groggily she recognized her stepfather's voice angrily shouting at her mother. Fearful, she slid out from the covers and made her way on tiptoe to the door of her mother's bedroom. She peered in and saw the two of them involved in some kind of argument. They stood face-to-face, her mother dressed in a nightgown, her stepfather obviously drunk as he jerked loose his shirt.

"Just get off my back," he snarled. "I'll stay out as long as I want anytime I please, and don't forget it."

"But people are talking. You don't know how foolish you make me feel, how hard it is for me to hold my head up while I pretend I don't know that you're out with another woman every night."

"What I do is no concern of yours."

"It is my concern," her mother cried. "I can't go on living a lie like this. I want a divorce."

Mason laughed coldly. "Of course you can have your divorce. As soon as you give me control of the company."

"No. I've got to protect Marla. It was her father's company. If I give it to you, she'll have nothing."

"That's her bad luck," he snapped.

"All right," her mother said, tightlipped. "If you want to make this difficult, I'll go ahead with the divorce and the whole world can find out about your philandering. You'll end up with nothing."

Then Mason's beefy hands had clamped down on her mother's shoulders, and he shook her like a rag doll. Marla was terrified, unable to tear her eyes away from her mother's pale face as Mason vented his anger. Then Marla's screams rang out, and they both stared at her in stupefied surprise.

Tears streamed down her cheeks. She couldn't stop crying. "I don't want the company," she screamed at them. "Just leave my mother alone. Please don't hurt her."

In an instant her mother's arms were around her, but Marla kicked and screamed to be freed. Far away, someone was calling her name over and over.

Suddenly her eyes flew open, and she saw Brent sitting on the bed, bending over her. He was holding her wrists together in one hand as she struggled. "Marla," he said sharply. "Wake up."

She blinked hard and looked around the room quickly to make sure of where she was. Then she looked up at Brent plaintively and was startled to see concern in his dark eyes. He released her wrists slowly and reached out to touch her cheek where the tears were still wet. "Are you all right?" he asked softly.

She nodded, swallowing hard. "It was just a nightmare."

"It must have been a terrifying one," he said. "You were crying and fighting me."

His eyes were still on her face and she looked down, her wet lashes dark against her pale cheek. "I'm all right now," she whispered.

Still he didn't move, and she felt her heart beating faster when she looked up at him again. Slowly he leaned closer to her, and at the last moment she closed her eyes with a heavy sigh. His lips claimed hers, gently at first, then more fiercely. She felt herself melting beneath his touch as his tongue explored her mouth and her own responded. She had a thirst for him that couldn't be slaked. Fresh from the terrors of her nightmare, she needed his comfort and closeness. Her arms twined around his neck, and his mouth dropped to her neck, his lips scorching her there. She felt his hand trace a line down her cheek, her throat, and then follow the lacy cup of her slip. She strained closer to him, wanting the warmth of his touch. Pressing her even nearer, his other hand tightened on her back. She let her head fall back, her blonde hair cascading down behind her, her arms clinging to his neck. He still nibbled at her throat, and she could hear his breathing quicken.

From the depths of her being she sighed his name, barely a whisper, yet he heard. She felt him shudder slightly. Gradually his breathing returned to normal, and he moved his lips from her throat. His hands were twined in her hair now, and reluctantly she raised her head to look at him, confusion in her eyes.

"It's time you got dressed for dinner," he said, not a trace of the passion she'd thought he was feeling, in his voice or face.

She stared at him as he stood up and straightened his tie. Was he playing some kind of game with her? He had just proved his control over her, and now he was ordering her to get ready for dinner. Was this Brent's way of convincing her she couldn't fight him?

She saw him glance down the length of her body, and she looked down, feeling suddenly embarrassed when she realized she was dressed only in a slip and that she had kicked off the cover during her nightmare. She felt color rise to her face and quickly climbed off the bed and headed toward the chair where she had put her suit.

"Are you blushing?" he asked in cool amusement as he caught her arm and turned her toward him.

Angrily she lowered her eyes and tried to turn her head, but he cupped her chin in one hand and swung her face around. "I can't imagine why you're embarrassed," he said relentlessly. "You should be used to having your lovers see you in less clothing than this."

"This is different," she muttered. "You're not my lover."

"At one time I was," he said softly.

"Let me go so I can get dressed," she said in rising nervousness.

With a short laugh he released her, and she hurried to the chair and picked up her suit.

"You're not wearing that to dinner tonight," he said, and she faced him defiantly, hands on hips.

"I most certainly am."

"I brought along something more suitable."

"Give it to one of your other lady friends—and I use the term 'lady' loosely. I don't want it."

He glared at her, then left the bedroom, and Marla sighed in relief. She had slipped into the skirt and was hastily buttoning the jacket when he came back. She turned with a start, her eyes going to the box in his hand.

"You'll wear this instead," he said shortly, tossing the box onto the bed.

"What gives you the right to pick out my clothes?" she demanded angrily.

"Someone has to do it," he said matter-of-factly. He indicated her suit. "That shapeless thing looks like a tweed garbage bag on you. If you want to hide the fact that you're an attractive woman, you're doing a fine job of it. And while we're on the subject of clothes, what were mine doing out in the hall?"

She smiled with acid sweetness. "I think that's clear enough. I don't intend sharing the same room with you. You've been evicted."

"For your information, I didn't intend spending the night here," he said grimly. "My bedrooms at home were being remodeled so with Karl's permission I spent a few nights here. I'd intended moving my things this morning, but I didn't have time."

She stared at him, taken aback. So he hadn't planned

on spending the night here after all.

"Now are you going to get out of that ridiculous suit?"

She shook her head. She had given enough ground for one day.

Shrugging, he took a step closer, and she instinctively backed up. Then she forced herself to stand still as he stopped in front of her. But she wasn't prepared when he reached out with both hands and grasped the front of her jacket. He gave a sudden jerk and the buttons went flying in all directions. She gasped and pulled the jacket closed across her slip as he stood back with satisfaction. "There," he said. "Now, unless you intend wearing your slip to dinner, I suggest you put on the dress I brought." He turned and walked calmly to the door, then stopped and faced her again. "And don't bother pinning your hair back in that matronly style. I promise, I won't be any too gentle pulling the pins out."

"You!" she hissed at him, but he only laughed and left the room, closing the door behind him.

CHAPTER
Three

MARLA STOOD FUMING after he'd left. She longed to defy him, to pull together the torn front of her suit, follow him into the other room, and coolly announce that she wasn't going to dinner with him, that she wasn't going anywhere with him until he learned to behave in a civilized manner.

But even as she thought it, she glanced down at the buttons scattered on the carpet and realized the futility of her resistance on this issue. Brent appeared determined to enforce his will. And she didn't care to lose another clash with him so soon. Already he was making her feel helpless against him.

Sighing heavily, she glanced at the closed door, then pulled off the jacket and skirt. Curious, she opened the box lying on the bed and held up the dress, blinking several times. It was beautiful.

She hesitated a moment, then slipped it on and zipped up the back. Slowly she turned to the mirror and surveyed her reflection. The chemise was a pale blue jersey that accented her eyes. It was gathered at the waist, then flowed into a soft, full skirt. The long sleeves had just enough fullness before they were gathered at the wrist. And where the neckline plunged into a deep vee there was a delicate lace insert in the palest blue. With her long blonde hair falling about her shoulders, she looked soft and feminine and better than she'd looked in months.

She turned from the mirror and took her brush, and out of habit pulled her hair sharply back. Then she remembered Brent's threat to yank out the pins. She stood debating over how much she should defy him, then decided she was too tired to fight anymore that night. She brushed her hair until it fell in becoming waves around her face and then slipped on her shoes. She picked up her purse and resolutely opened the door to the other room.

He was standing at the window, one hand in his pocket. He turned at the sound of the door, and they stared at each other wordlessly. His dark eyes seemed to burn into her as he inspected every inch of her slender form, and she forced herself to remain aloof under his scrutiny. "You look very attractive," he said at last, softly.

"Thank you," she answered curtly.

"We'll have to do something about those shoes another time," he said caustically as he moved from the window. She tightened her lips angrily but said nothing.

He helped her into her coat, then held the door for her. As he guided her to his car, she felt a tingle run through her at the touch of his hand on her arm, and she had to remind herself that this was all part of a business deal. She'd better watch herself, because tonight she needed all of her strength and intelligence. One didn't enter lightly into negotiations with Brent Stevens.

He took her to an expensive restaurant, and Marla wondered bitterly to herself if he would put the meal on his expense account. When they had finished the veal scallopini and wine, Brent ordered them each a cognac and sat back in his chair. "Have things been running smoothly at the Syracuse office?"

She looked at him in surprise. "Yes," she murmured.

"I imagine you've kept busy this last year," he said cryptically, and she stared at him, trying to read his expression.

"There's always something to do," she shrugged. "I keep busy."

He reached into his pocket and tapped out a cigarette, and Marla mentally braced herself. "I see the negotiations are about to begin," she said with a wry smile.

"The negotiations?"

She nodded toward the cigarette. "You always smoke before a difficult business deal. I always thought you were extremely self-disciplined to confine your smoking to those few occasions."

He squinted at her through the cigarette smoke, pausing to exhale before he spoke. "You're very observant."

"Apparently not observant enough where the business was concerned," she commented dryly.

"There's no way you could have known what Karl was up to," he said, surprising her with the warmth in his voice. "He was very careful to cover his tracks. No one would have known, if his little deal hadn't fallen through."

"Karl's been involved in disreputable dealings all his life. I should have checked on him, but..."

She trailed off, lowering her eyes, and he finished for her. "But you didn't want to come back to Quebec."

She nodded. "There was no need for you to leave in the first place," he said flatly. "I suppose you thought I was going to pursue you after you rejected me."

She didn't answer and knew he took her silence as agreement. In truth, she'd been more afraid that she would see him again and that her heart would skip a beat the way it was doing now.

"Marla." His voice was a command, and she raised her eyes to him slowly. "I don't hunt until I know for certain I can catch my quarry," he said quietly. His eyes locked with hers, and she read his meaning all too well there. She was his quarry, and he knew he had her at last.

He stamped out the cigarette, and she knew he was ready to come to terms. "I'm prepared to buy the stock, Marla," he said.

She twisted her napkin on her lap, hardly daring to look at him. "I called Jack," she said quietly. "He convinced me it has to be sold."

"I figured you'd run to him," Brent said coldly, and Marla read the disdain in his eyes. Her face burned as she remembered the lie she'd told him the year before.

"And I should have known you'd be thorough enough to send Jack a full financial report."

"It seemed necessary, considering he was the man you left me for. Is he still your lover, Marla, or are there others now?"

She flushed and started to retort angrily, but he stopped her. "No, don't tell me. I don't think I want to know about your sordid little affairs."

She burned with the urge to tell him it was all a lie, but the memory of that night a year ago and why she'd told him the lie kept her silent.

"I assume that since you've decided to agree to the sale, you've also agreed to the second condition."

"I don't understand why you insist on that," she said plaintively, studying his face for a sign of softening but seeing only hard determination.

"I've told you, Marla. You'd be an asset to me. And it will give me infinite satisfaction to know you're forced to give up your parade of lovers and pretend to be a faithful wife."

"What do you mean?" she asked hoarsely.

"I mean that if you so much as take a second glance

at another man, I'll insist that you be a real wife to me. Until you step out of line, Marla, you'll share my name only. But I warn you. The slightest provocation on your part and I'll consider it necessary to show you what a loving husband I am. That means that unless you want to share my bed, you'll have no lovers and you'll make no attempt to escape our marriage. Is that understood?" With a sardonic twist to his lips he crossed his arms over his chest and watched her.

Marla's eyes were wide and her face pale as she stared back at him. "But you said it would be a platonic marriage," she whispered.

"And it will be. But only if you don't break the rules. Now, do you accept the conditions?"

Desperate to escape his trap, Marla cast about for any lifeline she could grasp. "Surely I won't be expected to spend every moment with you," she said quickly.

"What do you mean?" His eyes narrowed speculatively.

"I mean that this marriage will probably be as boring to you as it will to me." She saw him frown angrily. "I suggest we agree that after a specified time we spend some time apart, a separation of sorts."

She met his gaze, hoping he couldn't read the desperation in her eyes. She knew he was watching her intently, judging how far he could push her.

"Perhaps we could reach an agreement on that," he said without emotion, and she swallowed in relief at this one concession. He leaned forward and sipped his cognac. "After one year of marriage you may leave Quebec for a while, without me."

She shook her head resolutely. "That's too long," she insisted. He was frowning again, but she pressed on. "It's three months until February and the Winter Carnival. Let me leave after that." She clenched her teeth to keep her lip from trembling as he looked down at his glass, considering what she'd said. At last he looked up, his eyes locking with hers. "Very well. After the Winter Carnival you may leave for a while."

"All right," she whispered.

He searched her face and saw her hesitation. "There's something else?"

"The company," she managed to blurt out. "Will I have any part in it?"

His hooded eyes regarded her closely, and her breath was suspended. He could invoke even greater revenge on her now. He could deny her any access to her father's company, or he could relegate her to a menial position where she would have to observe him from a distance. Either alternative would be unbearable.

"What did you have in mind?" he asked evenly.

She steeled herself and pressed on. "I can't stand by and watch from the sidelines," she said quietly. "That would be tantamount to a slow death. I want an active, important part in the direction of Stanford Electronics."

"Is that a demand?" he countered.

She flushed, well aware that she was in no position to make demands. "I'm afraid so," she said at last, her heart hammering. "You can't take my life away from me."

"I didn't intend to," he said quietly. "I had expected that you would remain as the de facto director of operations with the title of Vice-President in Charge of Production. I still have a great deal of responsibility at my own company, Daricom, which I haven't delegated elsewhere yet. And I'll need your invaluable assistance and experience to acquaint me with the operations at Stanford. Is that agreeable?"

She nodded. "Yes."

"Then you agree to all the conditions?" he repeated.

There was a charged silence between them, and Marla searched one last time for some sign that he might yet relent. But his eyes were cold and uncompromising, and she felt her last hope slip away.

"Yes," she finally whispered. She wasn't sure she'd said the word and less sure that he'd heard her, but his features relaxed somewhat and he picked up his cognac again.

"Good," he said. "The marriage will take place in two weeks. Is there anyone you want to invite?"

She laughed shortly. "Surely you're joking."

"You must really hate me," he said quietly, and she glanced at his face.

"It's just that I don't have anyone to invite," she murmured, wondering even as she said it why she was telling him the truth.

"You must have been lonely losing your father when you were only a baby and then your mother a few years ago."

"I suppose so," she said. "I don't really remember."

She found his gaze discomfiting and hurriedly sipped her cognac.

"There's a lot of pain under that cold exterior, isn't there?" he persisted, and Marla's hand trembled.

She set down her glass. "I'd like to go now, if you don't mind."

Brent stood up and moved around to help her to her feet. She felt almost giddy at the touch of his hand, but she blamed it on the cognac and the strain.

They drove to the hotel in silence, and Marla waited tensely while Brent got out of the car and came around to open her door. He took her up to her room and unlocked the door for her. Her heart was pounding as he turned to face her in the doorway. She was at the limits of her endurance, and she didn't think she could maintain her cold facade another minute. She prayed Brent would leave quickly—or she was liable to break down and cry in front of him.

"We haven't sealed our agreement," he said softly. She closed her eyes helplessly as she felt his strong hand gently lift her chin. His breath was warm on her mouth just before his lips claimed hers. Her hands clutched at his shirt as she swayed against him.

His mouth was hard and demanding, and her lips parted for him without resistance. It seemed her neck would break with the pressure of his kiss as he bent her head even farther back. When he finally released her and drew away, she was gasping for breath.

"Somehow you've grown even more beautiful in a year," he murmured as he bent his head again to nuzzle her ear.

She pushed against his chest. She had to stop him before she gave in completely. The intoxicating musky scent of his closeness, mingled with the sweet smell of cognac, was making her head spin. She backed up until she was pressed against the door frame and could go no farther.

"Still fighting me?" he whispered in amusement.

Marla was stung by his taunt, knowing how close she was to giving in completely. "I'll always fight you," she said. "Marriage will change nothing."

"We'll see," he said softly, tracing a line down her cheek with his finger. "Now get some sleep, and I'll pick you up in the morning for breakfast."

He handed her the room key, and she stammered, "good night."

Then he was gone and Marla closed the door, leaning all her weight against it in weariness. She suddenly felt so overwhelmed that she was unable to stop a flood of tears and stood there helplessly as they coursed down her cheeks.

Brent Stevens was back in her life again, and this time she wouldn't be able to escape him. A year ago all she had wanted was a quiet wedding, and the assurance she would spend the rest of her life with him. Now, ironically, that was just what she was going to have, but it was far from the paradise she'd once dreamed about. Because now she knew she'd never have his love. Their marriage would be a mockery, and she would be the one who suffered. Brent Stevens was determined to get revenge for her rejection, and he'd chosen the perfect method.

They'd never really known each other before, she told herself as she brushed away the tears and started washing up for bed. It had all happened so fast, with no time to think. She had met Brent at a dinner she had attended with Karl. There was an instant magnetism, and from that night on they had been inseparable. Karl had worried about the romance, and he'd continually warned her that Brent was not to be trusted. But Marla had dismissed his warnings as the graspings of a man afraid of losing his power in the company to a stranger.

Brent was the man she'd waited for all her life. Two months after they'd met, they had begun to talk about marriage. In bed, he'd shown her a tenderness and passion that had convinced her she'd finally found paradise. Those rough masculine hands were all gentleness when they kindled a fire on her skin that burned even after she was sated with his lovemaking.

Images of the gentle lover she'd known before came back to mock her now. They'd walked in the woods by a lake one early fall afternoon, silent because there was no need for words. His arm was around her shoulders, and she leaned against him. They stopped in the shadows of the trees, and he turned her to face him, then began to stroke her hair, all the time raining soft kisses on her upturned face.

"You're so beautiful," he said unsteadily, then he drew her slowly to the ground.

"Brent, someone will see us," she protested, but her voice carried no conviction, and her arms went around his neck.

"There's no one around for miles," he answered, then stilled any further protests with a gentle exploration of her parted lips with his tongue. Then lazily, contentedly, with supreme tenderness, he made love to her there on the soft bed of pine needles. His hands aroused her with feather touches until she was moaning softly, and his lips worshipped the pale curves and valleys of her body, nuzzling aside her clothes as carefully as though he were unwrapping a priceless gift.

Like sky and water meeting on the horizon, they blended together, their bodies entwined in the ultimate caress until a sunset of passion exploded within them.

It was the last time they'd made love.

Brent had a meeting that evening, and he'd told her with a promising smile that he'd see her the next day. Karl had volunteered to take her to dinner. He chose a nice restaurant, but when they entered, he suddenly stopped and said, "Maybe we'd better go somewhere else."

"Why?" Marla demanded.

"I hoped to spare you this," Karl said, "but perhaps it's better that you see for yourself."

He stepped aside, and Marla looked around the room curiously. Then she paled and drew back, her heart in her throat. Brent was sitting at a corner table just a few feet away with another woman, an attractive woman with short, reddish hair. As Marla stared in disbelief, he handed the woman a small box and she opened it, gasping in pleasure. Marla didn't want to look. Already she felt as though a knife was turning slowly inside her. But she forced herself to watch as the woman drew out a beautiful emerald ring surrounded by tiny diamonds and held it up to the light. She slipped it on her finger, and then Brent bent to kiss her...

Marla's vision was obscured as tears blinded her eyes. "Come on," Karl said in a solicitous voice. "I'll take you somewhere else."

"I want to tell him what I think of him," Marla said coldly, but Karl gripped her arm and pulled her away.

"No," he said sharply. "He'll just have some lie to

tell you, and there'll be a scene. It's best if we just leave."

In the end he had taken her home, saying he was sorry she'd had to find out that way but that he'd tried to warn her. He volunteered to make arrangements with the Syracuse office so she could work there.

Marla had been haunted all that night by visions of Brent and the red-haired woman. "I should have known," she sobbed into her pillow. "He's just like my stepfather, Mason." And when her tears were all gone, she'd vowed never to let any man into her heart again.

The next morning she had gathered the tattered remnants of her pride and gone to see Brent, determined to inflict as much pain on him as she could, in payment for her own wounded heart.

She had casually informed him that the fling was over and she was leaving for Syracuse. To his shocked inquiries she had said only that she hadn't meant for him to get so involved, that the whole thing had meant nothing to her.

"But you said you'd marry me," he protested in bewilderment.

"I never dreamed you were serious," she replied with a light laugh. "It was just a game to me. I thought you understood this was just something casual. I don't get involved in long-term affairs."

"Then I'm not the first?" Brent demanded angrily.

"Of course not." She laughed. "Nor the last."

She had never seen him so furious as he'd been then, and though she felt a sense of satisfaction that she'd paid him back in kind, it was a hollow victory.

"And I suppose you have another lover on the string in Syracuse?"

She'd glibly supplied Jack's name. He was practically the only person she knew in the Syracuse office, and she knew he would drop dead on the spot if he ever found out what she'd just told Brent. But the lie was necessary, she rationalized. It was the only way to sever the ties with Brent, to make the break cleanly though painfully.

To Brent's question if she had ever loved him, Marla had laughed coldly. "Love? If I feel anything for you, it's hate. I can't stand the sight of you."

She'd turned to go, but his angry voice had halted her. "Mark my words, Marla Stanford. One day we'll play this game again, and I'll be the one making the rules."

His words had made her shudder then, but she'd dismissed them as the empty threat of a jilted man. She should have known better. Brent Stevens always got what he wanted. And what he had wanted for a year now was to pay her back. He'd been thorough, all right. When he'd outlined his conditions, he'd sealed every avenue of escape. He'd known she would have no choice but to accept his proposal. And she was sure he'd enjoyed seeing her panic. He must have especially enjoyed her surrender this evening—first her forced agreement to his terms and then her physical surrender in his arms. He knew she found him attractive, and it amused him to use that against her.

She crawled into bed, exhausted, drained of all emotion. There was no use trying to get out of the wedding. The only concession she'd managed to gain was a temporary separation after Winter Carnival. She would cling to that promise and use all of her strength to fight Brent. It was going to be a long, difficult battle. She knew she could expect no gentleness from him now.

She fell into an uneasy sleep, pursued in her dreams by her stepfather as he paraded one woman after another in front of her tearful mother. And then Mason turned into Brent, and on his arm was the red-haired woman. In her dream Marla began crying, and Brent laughed.

CHAPTER
Four

A KIND OF numbness filled Marla during the next two weeks before the wedding. She kept outwardly calm and cool, allowing Brent to lead her through all the preparations, but inside she was churning.

There were papers to sign for the stock transfer, mounds of paperwork to process transferring control of the company, and a million and one other details that Marla was too dazed to take much note of.

Her single act of defiance came the day Brent took her to pick out her trousseau in Syracuse. She had sewn the buttons back on the jacket he had ripped that first night, and now she wore that suit and the same dowdy shoes. She greeted him with a cool smile, enjoying the irritation that flickered across his face. "Determined to make a last stand, are you?" he muttered under his breath as he guided her to the taxi. She winced at the grip of his hand on her arm, but resolutely kept the frozen smile on her face.

Once inside the store, he coolly and efficiently guided

the clerk through a selection of dresses and pants suits, sending Marla into the dressing room to try on some and arrogantly taking the others without even consulting her.

Inwardly fuming, Marla felt like a dumb mannequin being paraded for his appraisal. After he gave his stamp of approval to the final outfit, a silk blouse with lace collar and a wool skirt that she had to admit to herself was stunning, Marla wandered over to a counter displaying pajamas and grinned to herself. Picking up a package, she turned to Brent with a sweet smile.

"I think I ought to take this too," she said.

"A flannel nightgown?" he asked, one eyebrow cocked warily.

"Of course, dear," she cooed. "You know how cold the nights in Quebec can get. And I have a feeling our honeymoon will be especially chilly."

Brent ground his teeth in anger, and Marla suppressed a laugh as the salesclerk hastily cleared her throat in embarrassment and hurried to take the package from Marla. "I'll just wrap your things for you," she said nervously, bustling away.

"And I'll go change," Marla said brightly, feeling Brent's eyes boring into her back as she languidly made her way back to the dressing room.

But her triumph turned to dismay as she looked around and realized that her old suit and shoes weren't anywhere around. She poked her head out of the curtain to make sure she was in the right stall, then tentatively looked out the entrance to the rooms.

"Something wrong, my dear?" Brent asked suavely, and Marla eyed him suspiciously.

"Where are my clothes?" she demanded.

"You're wearing them," he said innocently.

"You know what I mean." She knotted her hands at her sides in anger.

"You must mean those old rags you were wearing," he said, the silky smile never leaving his face. "I had the saleslady throw those away."

"How dare you!" she fumed. "My shoes too?"

"That's right, my dear. She's gone to get you another pair. Let's see now. You're about a nine or ten, aren't you?" he asked, his eyes crinkling in amusement as he deliberately let his eyes drop to her stockinged feet, which were curling in anger and embarrassment.

She glared at him, her eyes shooting daggers, as she saw the salesclerk returning with a pair of black heels in her hands. "You deliberately tried to embarrass me by having her throw away my clothes," she hissed.

"Fair play, my dear," he said, his eyes burning into her. "You tried to do the same with the flannel night-gown."

Color rose to her face. He was still one step ahead of her.

The clerk was holding out the shoes and motioning Marla to a nearby chair. "Try these on, honey. The gentleman knew your size." Marla sank down in the chair and looked at the shoes, then glanced at Brent in surprise. They were a size six, a perfect fit. Surprising her even more, Brent grinned at her, his teeth gleaming as he laughed softly.

Marla quickly ducked her head to hide her own smile. He was so disarming that he always managed to catch her off guard. She slipped on the shoes, then stood up to survey her reflection in the mirror. She had to admit she looked attractive, and she self-consciously raised her hand to her hair falling about her face.

Brent's reflection appeared just behind hers, and she watched him in the mirror, struck by the admiration on his face. She swallowed hard as he reached out to gently stroke her hair. "You look lovely," he said quietly. "I think our next stop should be the jewelry department. I saw a pair of gold earrings that will look terrific on you."

The smile faded from Marla's face. "No jewelry," she said curtly. He seemed surprised, and she quickly moved away from him to hide her unhappiness. Brent's offer only reminded her of the pain she'd suffered the year before, seeing him give another woman jewelry. Brent was like her stepfather, Mason. Jewelry appeased a woman, dazzled her so that she didn't see what the man giving the gift was really like. As long as a woman was blinded by gold and silver, her husband could stray as far as he wanted. To accept jewelry from Brent meant surrender, and she wasn't going to give in to him, no matter how charming he might be.

He went with her to the bank, where she closed out her account while Brent idly wandered into the lobby. The clerk punched up the account in the computer, then said, "Both accounts, Miss Stanford?"

Confused, Marla looked down at her checkbook. "I don't remember any other account," she said.

"A savings account," the woman said. "You have a balance of nine thousand dollars in it."

Marla searched her memory. She couldn't recall ever opening a savings account at this bank. Then she remembered the account her mother had opened in her name when she was a little girl. She and her mother had moved to Syracuse shortly after the last fight Marla had witnessed, and Mason had stayed in Quebec. Her mother had brought her to this bank on every birthday to deposit some of her cash presents in the account. She'd understood little of money matters then, and she was surprised now to learn that there was so much money in the account.

"Would you like to close this account as well?" the woman asked again.

Marla paused and then glanced quickly behind her at Brent. He was absorbed in a magazine, and she turned back to the clerk. "No," she said. "I think I'd like to leave this account here. But I'm changing my mailing address."

She quickly filled out a card and handed it back to

the woman. The statements would be sent to the Syracuse office instead of her apartment, and Brent would never see them. She would pick up the bankbook when she moved the last of her things out of her apartment. It had to be in the drawer with her personal papers.

"Are you about ready?"

She jumped at the sound of Brent's voice and turned to him, her eyes wide. "In a minute," she stammered.

He stood beside her, waiting as the woman finished making out a cashier's check for the closing balance in the checking account, and Marla fidgeted nervously. If he found out about the account she wasn't closing, he would no doubt insist she transfer the money with the rest.

Marla took the cashier's check with trembling fingers and thanked the clerk, hurrying away before anything else was said.

When they were in the taxi on the way to her apartment, Brent said, "You seem nervous. Is anything wrong?"

"No," Marla said quickly. "I guess it's just all these things that have to be done before the wedding." The last word came out almost a whisper, and she bit her lip, hoping he wouldn't take the opportunity to gloat over the fact that she was marrying him against her will.

"I suppose it must be difficult for you," he said slowly. "I'd thought it would be easier if we were married as quickly as possible, but if you need more time we can postpone the wedding."

Cautiously she turned to look at him, to see if he was sincere. He was staring straight ahead, and though his chiseled features seemed as inflexible as ever, there was a softening about the eyes. He turned toward her, and their eyes met briefly. "Do you want more time, Marla?"

She lowered her gaze quickly and murmured, "I suppose there's no point in waiting."

"If you mean I won't change my mind, you're right.

A postponement would be only that—a postponing of the inevitable. We'll be married, whether it's in a week or a month."

She looked out the window, her thick lashes veiling the anger that smoldered in her eyes. "Then I'd just as soon get it over with quickly," she countered coldly.

There was the briefest pause, and then he said in a low voice filled with amusement, "It won't be over then, my dear. It will only be beginning."

"Until the Winter Carnival," she muttered through clenched teeth. To her relief he said nothing, and she stared out the window until the cab pulled up in front of her apartment building.

The morning of the wedding Marla woke in her apartment with a feeling of dread. She longed to flee, to get as far away from Brent Stevens as she could, but she had no place to go. He had terminated the lease on her apartment, and already the vacancy had been filled. In fact, a woman was moving in that afternoon. The furniture was to stay with the new tenant, and Brent had arranged for the rest of Marla's belongings to be shipped to Quebec. She had spent the last two weeks shuttling between Quebec and Syracuse, tying up the loose ends of her old life and trying not to think about her new one.

Feeling trapped, Marla sank back under the covers and pulled them over her head. Somehow she had hoped something would happen before today to save her. But all along she had known Brent would let nothing stand in his way. She gritted her teeth in frustration.

Swinging her feet over the side of the bed, she pulled on her short terry-cloth robe. Her feet fumbled for the warmth of her furry slippers, and she padded into the kitchen to make coffee. Her legs were cold, and she wished she'd thought to leave a full-length robe in the apartment. But a warm robe wasn't the only thing missing, she discovered ruefully. All her clothes and dishes had been packed away and shipped off to Canada, she realized with dismay as she opened the cupboards. She was muttering under her breath, cursing Brent's thoroughness, when there was a knock on the door. Probably the new tenant, all bright-eyed and ready to move in, she thought irritably. Marla opened the door a crack and peered out, blinking hard when she saw Brent standing there, a paper bag in his hand.

"What are you doing here?" she demanded. "I'm supposed to meet you at the rectory."

"That's not a very fitting greeting for the groom," he replied cheerfully. "Besides, I brought you some coffee. In case you hadn't noticed, I had your things packed up and sent ahead."

"No, I hadn't noticed," she said testily. "I thought I'd turned into Old Mother Hubbard while I was asleep."

"My, aren't you grumpy before your morning coffee," he said in mock surprise. "It's good I'm finding these things out before the wedding. Now, are you going to let me in, or shall I get a straw so you can sip this coffee through the door?"

Marla slipped the chain off the door and stood back as Brent sauntered in. Wordlessly, she led him to the kitchen and plopped down on a stool at the breakfast bar, watching through half-closed lids as he pulled two cups of coffee from the bag and sat down on a stool beside her.

"Drink up," he said. "We have to get going."

"What's the big hurry?" she muttered, savoring the first sip.

"We have an appointment with a minister," he reminded her.

"And you're my armed escort?" she said. "Where are the handcuffs, sheriff? Did you really think I'd leave you waiting at the altar?"

"The thought had occurred to me," he said quietly.

"I don't welch on my agreements," she said.

"I certainly hope not," he answered. She heard the low tone of amusement in his voice and turned to glare at him. She saw his flinty eyes appraising her, and she flushed vividly as she realized that the short robe had crept up her legs as she sat, revealing a long, slender expanse of thigh. Hastily she stood up and tugged the robe down as far as she could. "I think I'll get dressed now," she muttered, stalking to the bathroom with as much dignity as she could muster with his eyes following her.

She washed her face, then padded back to the bedroom and yanked open her closet door, wondering what was left for her to wear. But it seemed he'd thought of that too. There was a solitary garment bag hanging there, and she pulled it out, knowing full well it was her wedding dress. He'd orchestrated everything else so far. Naturally he'd chosen her wedding dress as well.

The only alternative was the pants suit she'd worn the day before, and she knew he wouldn't let her leave for their wedding in that. Grimly, she slipped off the robe and went into the bathroom to put on her underclothes and slip. When she came back, she stood staring at the garment bag on the bed, then unzipped it and pulled out the dress. Like the other clothes he had picked out for her, this was beautiful, and if possible, even more feminine. Everything he had chosen was designed to accent her womanliness. She slipped on the dress and carefully fastened the fabric buttons that went up the front. She ran her hand tentatively down to straighten the dress. It was soft pink cashmere and clung gently to her slender curves. The long sleeves were fitted and the neckline was edged with a hint of pink lace.

She took her brush and ran it vigorously through her hair until it gleamed. She didn't even care when the brush caught in her hair. She tugged viciously, tears of rage and pain coming to her eyes.

She didn't hear him come into the room, and she froze

when he reached out and began gently disentangling the brush from her hair. She stood still, feeling like a puppet as he continued brushing her hair. "The finishing touch," he said quietly, setting down the brush and holding out a spray of tiny pink roses and baby's breath. She watched in the mirror as he pinned it in her hair, and then his hands dropped to her shoulders. "You look beautiful," he said softly.

"I'm glad I meet with your approval," she said coldly. "But then, how could it be otherwise? You've seen to everything."

"Now what's wrong?" he asked, frowning.

"Nothing. Why should I complain? After all, this is my wedding day. You've chosen my dress, the minister, my trousseau. You've taken care of everything. You've treated me like a doll, to be pushed and dressed and taken where you want."

He turned her around to face him, and she stared up at him angrily as a cold smile spread over his face. "This is exactly what you want, isn't it?" she demanded sharply. "To make me feel like a puppet in your hands?"

"That's right, my dear," he said, a gleam of mockery in his eyes.

"You aren't even going to deny it?"

He shrugged. "Why should I? I've made no secret of what I want."

"And what you want is to make me miserable, isn't it?" she asked in a low voice.

"That's entirely up to you," he said enigmatically. "I want you to be my wife. Anything else is up to you."

"Nothing's up to me," she hissed. "You leave me no choice in anything. You wouldn't even allow me to choose my own wedding dress. How can I help but be miserable?"

"Ah, that's it," he said in amusement. "It's the dress, isn't it? You're angry because I chose it for you. Don't you like it?"

"The dress is beautiful," she said, then stammered, "I mean, it's all right. It makes no difference to me anyway."

"But it seems it does make a difference to you. Is the color wrong? Certainly you didn't expect a white wedding gown, did you?"

"What are you talking about?"

"Surely you don't expect me to believe you're entitled to wear white on your wedding day," he demanded in cold amusement. "Not after you made a point of informing me of your legion of lovers."

Without thinking, she swung her hand at him, but he caught her wrist tightly and pulled her to him. "Perhaps I should have picked a scarlet dress," he said in a low, threatening voice, "but I decided to spare you that embarrassment."

He easily caught the other wrist as she furiously pounded on his chest. He swung her hands behind her back, and when she was pinned helplessly against his lean body, he brought his mouth down forcefully on hers, crushing the breath from her. When he finally raised his head, she was close to fainting. "Remember, from now on there won't be any other lovers, Marla," His grip tightened on her wrists, making her wince. "Now put on your shoes and try to look happy. Remember, this is your wedding day." He released her and turned on his heel, stopping at the doorway to look back at her. She was pale, her blue eyes pools of wounded pride as she stood rubbing her wrists. "I'll get your coat," he said in a softer voice, and then he disappeared.

Slowly she went to the closet, where she found the pair of white heels he'd left for her. She'd discovered something about Brent that she hadn't realized before. What infuriated him more than the fact that she'd jilted him was the string of lovers she'd led him to believe existed. She would remember that, and use it against him when the chance came. He might have the upper hand now, but she had found a chink in Brent Stevens's armor. She was going to make sure he got as little satisfaction from this forced marriage as she did.

They were married in the rectory of a small church near Marla's apartment, a church Brent had chosen. Marla remembered little of the ceremony except the relentless pressure of Brent's hand on hers and the simple gold wedding band he slipped on her finger. They were pronounced man and wife, and Brent tilted her face up to his and gave her a soft lingering kiss under the benevolent smile of the minister.

Afterward, they drove away in a rented car. Marla leaned back wearily against the seat. She must have slept, because the next thing she knew she was jolted awake as the car came to a halt. "Are we stopping for gas?" she asked sleepily, and Brent laughed.

"No, my dear, we're stopping for our honeymoon."

"What?" she cried, suddenly wide awake. "Where are we?"

"Horseshoe Falls," he replied with a grin. "I hear all the newlyweds visit here."

"We're not staying here, are we?" Marla ventured in utter dismay.

"What's wrong, my dear?" he teased her. "Isn't it romantic enough for you? Actually we'll only spend the night here. Tomorrow we're catching a pleasure boat to travel up the St. Lawrence to Quebec."

"But you promised," she began, then faltered, not sure how to continue. Surely he wasn't going back on his word now that they were married.

"If you mean our marital relationship," he said with a smile, "the answer is no. Ours will remain a marriage in name only. But it would appear strange to everyone if we didn't take some kind of honeymoon. I thought you might enjoy this trip."

Without waiting for her to reply, he got out of the car and came around to open her door. "I sent our luggage ahead," he said, helping her out of the car. "It's waiting for us in the cabin."

Dazed, she allowed him to lead her toward the cluster of cabins a little distance from their car. Marla looked around and realized they were near the falls. She could hear the rushing water nearby.

Brent registered them in the office, and the male clerk gave them a warm smile as he handed them the key. "Congratulations, sir," he said to Brent. "Best wishes to you both."

Brent smiled sardonically as he took the key and ushered Marla toward the door.

Once in their cabin, Marla wandered around with her coat still clutched around her. "Are you cold?" Brent asked. "I'll start a fire." He built a roaring blaze in the stone fireplace that took up one wall of the cabin, and she warmed her hands in front of it. He helped her slip off her coat and then came back to stand beside her. She stared at the flames as he slowly removed the flowers from her hair and tossed them on a chair. Then gently he stroked her hair. "Do you want to get some rest?" he asked. "You seemed pretty tired on the way here."

"I'm fine," she murmured.

"Would you like to look at the falls, then?"

She shrugged, and he said, "I'll get you a cup of coffee, and then we'll go."

Half an hour later they were walking along the edge of the gorge of Horseshoe Falls, and Marla stopped to stare down at the swirling water below. The roar of the water was deafening, and she stared out at the horseshoe-shaped gorge where the magnificent falls cascaded to the water below. She felt Brent's arm encircle her waist, and she unconsciously touched the wedding band on her finger.

"It's beautiful, isn't it?" he said.

She nodded. "Such power."

"Look." He pointed below, and she followed his gaze. Just emerging from the heavy mist created by the falls was the *Maid of the Mist,* looking like a ghost ship leaving the fog. They stood watching the boat, and Marla sighed deeply, feeling herself in the presence of a strong force. It wasn't just the falls, awesome as it was. She was locked in some other struggle, fighting for what, she didn't know. Maybe it was freedom from Brent and the strong will he was determined to force on her. Perhaps it was an internal struggle to deny herself the feelings she had fought against all her life. Whatever it was, she knew she would soon need every ounce of her strength.

They had a late dinner in their cabin that night, steak and champagne by candlelight, and all through the meal Marla was uncomfortably aware of Brent's masculine presence. She could feel his flinty gray eyes on her, and she kept her eyes on her own champagne glass, sipping slowly. When they had returned to the cabin, he had changed into a red-plaid flannel shirt and casual slacks, while Marla had dried her mist-laden hair in front of the fire and slipped into wool slacks and a sweater.

"Do you still enjoy sketching?" he asked her unexpectedly, and she looked up in surprise.

"Yes, I do."

"I'm glad. You were very good at it."

She looked down again, embarrassed by his praise. "It relaxes me."

He set down his champagne glass and stood up. "I brought along a sketch pad and some ink if you'd like to have them."

"Why, thank you." A quick smile flitted across her face, and he stared down at her until she looked away. He went to his luggage and returned with the pad and ink and some pens, which he set on the table before her. "Thank you," she said again, happiness shining in her eyes.

"Go ahead and draw now if you'd like." He picked up his glass and went to stand in front of the fire, his back to her.

She closed her eyes for a moment, envisioning the

falls again, then set about putting what she remembered on paper. She worked for half an hour, engrossed in the scene taking shape before her, and didn't notice that Brent had come to stand behind her.

She stopped at last and critically evaluated what she'd done. It wasn't bad, but she was rusty, not having drawn in almost a year.

"It's beautiful. You've captured all the grandeur of Horseshoe Falls."

She started at the sound of his voice, then hastily pushed the paper aside. "It's not quite right. Maybe after I get another look at it tomorrow."

"No, you've got it now," he said in a low voice. "The boat coming out of the mist is perfect." He seemed lost in thought as he stared down at the drawing. "It's a lot like you, Marla. So much hidden. What's beneath all that beautiful mist?" He tangled his fingers in her hair, and she stiffened even as she felt a hypnotic warmth spreading through her.

"It's only a drawing," she said nervously, "and not a very good one at that. I should throw it in the fire." She made a move to do just that, but he caught her arm and slowly drew her to her feet.

"I want to keep it," he said quietly. "I don't have any of your drawings, and I'd like to have this one."

"All right," she whispered, unable to look away from his compelling eyes.

Suddenly she was aware of the warmth emanating from him and felt irresistibly drawn to it. She let him pull her even closer, his arms wrapping around her. He kissed her hair, gently at first and then with growing urgency. Fire was licking at her veins as he tilted her face up to his, and she offered her full lips to him willingly. He claimed them with a fierce passion that left her trembling in his arms.

She clung to his neck, giving herself up to him, pressed against his soft shirt and the hard muscles beneath it. She gave a shuddering sigh as he raised his head from hers and stared down into her eyes. She knew he could read the desire there, but she was powerless to hide it.

Gently he cradled her head to his chest, and then she felt his arms fall away from her. She raised her head quizzically and saw the old mocking light in his eyes.

"It's late, Cinderella," he said softly. "You'd better go to bed before you turn into a pumpkin."

She searched his face for a sign of the passion she had been sure he was feeling only a moment ago, but his eyes gazed back at her like flinty steel. Had he deliberately made sport of her, teasing her into surrender, then enjoying his victory? The bruising embrace had probably been part of his revenge, a ploy to make her admit she wanted him before he shoved her aside. His praise of her ink drawing had no doubt been part of the plan to melt her resistance.

Feeling foolish and used, she pulled away from him and backed up to the table. "I'll go change," she murmured tightly, feeling color rise to her face as he continued to watch her lazily. She hurried toward the bedroom and pulled open her suitcase, rummaging angrily for a nightgown. She found the flannel nightgown she'd insisted on getting for her trousseau and felt cold satisfaction. He wouldn't find her so easily manipulated from now on.

When she was dressed for bed, she burrowed down into the covers and curled tightly into a ball. She opened her eyes cautiously a while later when Brent came into the bedroom. By the pale light filtering through the window she could see his outline, and when he took off his robe she realized he was wearing only pajama bottoms. The firm muscles of his torso flexed as he tossed the robe on the chair, and she couldn't help remembering the feel of those strong arms around her just a short while ago.

She hardly breathed as he walked past the bed, but

he went to the second bed and got in. She wondered what she would have done if he had gotten into bed with her, and then she pushed that thought from her mind and tried to go to sleep.

But memories kept intruding on her, memories from a year before when she and Brent had lain in each other's arms. Minutes had stretched into pleasure-laden hours as his hands gently caressed her body into burning desire. The soft love words he had murmured to her were an age-old beckoning that she had succumbed to with willing passion, her own undisguised need moving him to cradle her possessively. She could still hear his voice whispering hoarsely, "my love, my love," as he melded their bodies into one fierce flame.

And now, on their wedding night, she lay cold and alone, forever denied the warmth and passion she'd found in Brent's arms, the love she'd once believed was real.

The tender lover was gone, and in his place was a cruel stranger.

When she opened her eyes the next morning, she looked cautiously out from under the covers, but Brent was already up and gone. She went hurriedly into the bathroom and put on her clothes, a soft corduroy pants suit in pale mauve. She did her hair in one thick braid and then went to the living room to warm herself in front of the fire.

Brent must be in the cabin office, she decided. She put on her coat and went out the cabin door, jamming her hands in the pockets. She could hear the sound of the falls, even here, and she felt drawn to them. She quickly crossed the lawn until she came to a rocky slope and stood there staring at the mist rising in the distance. Brent had said she was like the mist, her innermost self hidden. She closed her eyes and listened to the roar of the water. It was ironic. Brent had hidden more about himself than she had. He was like the falls—powerful and beautiful, but also treacherous to anyone who got too close. She wasn't going to let herself be drawn near enough to be destroyed.

"What are you doing out here?" She turned at the sound of his sharp question, still lost in thought.

"I just wanted to hear the water again," she said.

"When I got back to the cabin and found you were gone, my first thought was that you'd run away," he said.

"I said I'd stay with you until after the Winter Carnival, and I meant it," she said stiffly.

"And you know the price if you don't," he reminded her in a low voice. "Although after last night, maybe you're more willing to forfeit your part of the agreement. As I recall, we were very good together once."

She flushed angrily at his reference to her surrender. "You shouldn't find it so surprising that I'd enjoy a man's touch. After all, I've grown accustomed to it, having experienced it frequently." She glared at him, hoping she'd hit home. But the only sign he gave of anger was a clenching of his jaw.

"It's time to catch the boat," he said coldly. "We'd better go."

He grasped her arm and pulled her back toward the cabin, and Marla mentally steeled herself. She had weathered her wedding night, but the rest of the honeymoon stretched before her. She hoped the boat trip wouldn't prove as unnerving as Horseshoe Falls.

He stood by her side at the railing as they traveled up Lake Ontario, past forts from a more turbulent era. "The original homes were burned by the Americans in 1813," Brent said, pointing toward a cluster of beautiful houses on the shore. "The Canadians have always proved to be fierce fighters when necessary."

He pointed out other landmarks to her until she grew cold, and then he took her inside for coffee and eggs. They returned to the railing as the boat began its mazelike passage through the Thousand Islands. Postage-stamp islands dotted the waterway like dollops of whipped cream, some sporting houses and families, others forested and uninhabited.

"They're like something out of a fairy tale," Marla said, lost in contemplation as she stared over the railing.

"You haven't seen much of Canada, have you?" Brent asked curiously.

"No. My mother and I left when I was little."

"Then I'll have to show it to you. We'll start with Quebec."

A woman of about sixty had come to stand near them at the rail, and now she turned to Brent, her eyes eager as she said, "Quebec? You know it well, monsieur?"

"Oui," he replied, smiling, and her animated face lit up. She immediately launched into French, and Brent laughed, nodding and agreeing with her, answering in French himself. Marla listened and watched, fascinated. The woman indicated the St. Lawrence, and her face sobered as she said something. Brent too looked reflective as he stared off into the distance before answering her. Then he put his arm around Marla and drew her forward, introducing her to the woman. "Marla, Madame Bouchet."

"I'm so pleased to meet you, Madame Stevens," the woman said with an engaging smile. "Do you speak French also?"

"I'm sorry, no," Marla said.

"Such a pity."

"Never fear, Madame Bouchet," Brent laughed. "Eventually I'll remedy that."

The woman took her leave, and Marla turned to Brent. "What did she say to you? You both seemed so serious."

"We were talking about the old ways of the Québecois—French Canadians—and how things have changed."

"Are things that different?" Marla asked curiously.

Brent shrugged. "Change is inevitable. But it isn't

always good. Madame Bouchet is on her way back to Quebec City after a long absence in the States. She's proud of her heritage, and she fears she'll no longer fit in. Her grandchildren no longer know any French, and her children have deserted their family church. The family in general, once so important to French Canadians, has deteriorated. Even the land has changed. The French Canadians have always loved the land, and now industry and so-called progress pollute even that. I'm afraid one day even the St. Lawrence may be choked to death by progress."

"That's an unusual sentiment for a businessman," Marla observed softly.

Brent turned to her, and she saw a proud light in his gray eyes. "But I'm a French Canadian first, a businessman second," he said quietly. "I don't advocate separatism, but I also don't want my heritage to die."

Marla nodded slowly. "It's a rich and beautiful heritage," she agreed. Shaking the reflective mood, she said, "Then perhaps we should start my French lessons, monsieur."

"All right, *ma petite,*" Brent laughed.

"*Ma petite?*" she repeated uncertainly.

His face sobered for a moment as his gaze lingered on her. "A term of endearment meaning 'my little one'," he explained. "I think it suits you. So often you remind me of a little girl, so shy and vulnerable. And then, like a butterfly, you turn into a beautiful woman before my eyes." He smiled wryly. "Enough of that. First, this is the boat, *le bateau.*"

"*Le bateau,*" she repeated, but her mind was still on his other words. *Ma petite.* The sound of them was like a caress, making her flesh tingle.

CHAPTER
Five

BRENT'S CAR WAS waiting for them when they got off
the boat at Quebec City, and he drove them silently to
his home, soon to be Marla's home too.

The honeymoon had passed surprisingly quickly for
Marla, and she had to admit she had enjoyed it. They
had gotten off the boat to sightsee in Montreal as well
as in some of the quaint, small towns along the St. Lawrence. By day Marla had listened to Brent's stories about
Canadian history and the seaway, and she'd picked up
more French words as he continued to tutor her. At night
they retired to their separate beds. The passion he had
aroused in her on their wedding night was not repeated;
indeed, not even mentioned again. Still, there was an
undercurrent between them, a strong force that she tried
to resist.

Now she glanced at his profile as he drove. There had
been an uneasy silence between them since they had
disembarked from the boat. For the past several days
they had been surrounded by other people, but now they

were going to be alone and they would be on Brent's own territory. Marla knew she was going to be at a disadvantage, and she wasn't looking forward to it.

He drove into the suburbs, and soon they were in the midst of the farmland outside the city. They came to a long country lane lined with pine trees, and Marla sat up as Brent turned onto it.

Fields stretched out on either side of the lane, lying fallow now with a covering of snow. They rounded a curve in the lane, and Marla saw a large farmhouse of frame and stone standing starkly against the gray sky, lush evergreens surrounding it.

"It's lovely," Marla whispered, awed by the simple beauty of the house.

She turned as the car stopped in front and saw Brent's eyes on her. "I'm glad you like it," he said. "I've done a lot of work inside, renovating it."

"Is this all your farm?" she asked.

"Yes, although I don't do any farming myself right now. But maybe one day. I have other people who farm it for me at present."

He helped her out of the car and took her arm as they followed the cobblestone walk toward the house. He swung open the massive, oak double doors, and she stepped gingerly inside, looking around in wonder. Hand-carved beams graced the high ceilings, giving the house a rustic look. She walked farther into the foyer, past a marble-topped stand with an old mirror mounted above it, and surveyed the kitchen in front of her. The floor was tiled in a black and white pattern that set off white walls covered on the upper half with gingham wallpaper. An enormous butcher-block work table formed the focus of attention in the center, with copper-bottom pans suspended above it. A small, informal eating alcove adjoined the kitchen, its maple table and chairs inviting a lingering cup of coffee.

Marla turned to the left and stepped into the living

room, which was papered in a deep blue print. A stone fireplace spanned the far wall, a primitive-style oil painting mounted above the marble mantel. The furniture was arranged for comfort, an overstuffed blue couch and leather chairs around the fireplace. Behind them a long coffee table was set with a decanter and wine glasses.

Marla turned and saw Brent standing in the doorway, his hands jammed in his coat pockets, observing her. "What do you think?" he asked.

"You did a wonderful job," she said with genuine admiration. "It's absolutely gorgeous, but homey too."

He smiled at her approval. "Would you like to see the upstairs? I'll bring our things up."

She nodded and followed him to the foyer, where their bags were lined up. He had just picked up two of them when a short, stout older man bustled in from a door off the hallway and stopped in surprise. "Monsieur Stevens!" he cried. "I had no idea you'd be here today. Here, let me help you."

"Thank you, Henri. May I introduce my wife, Marla."

The man's eyes lit up, and he clasped his hands together as he approached her. "This is indeed a pleasure, madame. May I be the first to wish you a long, happy life here in your new home."

"Thank you, Henri," Marla said, a little taken aback. Brent hadn't told her he employed any servants.

The little man hurried up the wooden staircase ahead of them, carrying a load of bags, while Brent and Marla followed with the rest.

"Henri, please put madame's things in here," Brent said, indicating the first room to the left. "Marla, if you'll come with me, I'll show you the rest of the upstairs." She followed him down the hall into the next room on the left. "This is the master bedroom," he said. "I'll be sleeping here." He put his luggage on the floor, and she stood awkwardly, embarrassed at his reference to the separate rooms. She looked around to avoid his eyes and was impressed by the soft brown colors accented by a warm yellow rug and small brick fireplace. He threw his coat on the mahogany canopy bed, and Marla moved toward the door.

"I guess I'll go unpack my things," she said.

"You can go this way," he said, indicating another door beside the bed. She moved toward it, realizing it adjoined her own bedroom. He saw her staring at the door and said with an amused smile, "I doubt this door will be necessary in the future, but it might be convenient at the moment."

She flushed and followed him into the room where Henri was arranging a vase of flowers on the dresser. "Thank you, Henri," Brent said. "That will be all for now."

"Shall I prepare dinner for you and madame?"

"Thank you, but no. Marla and I can whip up something for ourselves. I imagine she'll want to get acquainted with the kitchen."

"Very good, sir." With a deferential nod, Henri left, and Marla fingered the flowers. Violets again.

"I hope you won't mind Henri's presence," Brent said. "He'd planned to retire this winter and move south, but I asked him to stay on for a couple more months until we get settled in. I think you'll find his help invaluable."

"I'm sure I will," Marla murmured, her eyes on the flowers.

"I'll leave you to your unpacking now. Come on over when you're done, and I'll show you the other rooms. Then we can get some dinner."

She nodded, and he left through the same door. Marla sighed and turned from the flowers. The room was very feminine, and with a pang she wondered what other women had been here before her. She pushed aside the eyelet curtains and looked out across the fields, so cold and forbidding that she shivered slightly. She felt alone and abandoned here with no one but Brent. But at least her prison was comfortable.

She unpacked her luggage, admiring the oak dressers with their ornate brass pulls, and then she looked about for her sketches. Marla had drawn every day on the boat, usually as Brent lounged nearby. She had packed the drawings before they left the boat, but now she wondered if they hadn't been left behind.

She dawdled a while, reluctant to be alone with Brent again, but she was hungry, so she went to the door joining their rooms and tapped on it lightly. He called for her to come in, and Marla entered his bedroom.

He was sitting in the chair by the fireplace, but at her entrance he put down the magazine he was reading and stood up. He was polite but distant as he showed her the other upstairs rooms, then led her downstairs to the kitchen. Henri had retired for the night to his own quarters, and Marla and Brent were alone.

"I had Henri bring in some ham and potato salad," he said. "I thought we might have a simple meal."

"That's fine," she said. "I'll get some plates." She went through the cupboards, familiarizing herself with their contents, and came across a set of white stoneware. She got out two plates and two plain glasses as he carried ham and other containers to the table in the alcove.

He held her chair for her, then brought a bottle of wine to the table. "I guess I got the wrong glasses for wine," she said, but he smiled. "These will do just fine."

It was a quiet meal of ham, potato salad, cheese, and rolls, and they sipped their wine reflectively as the stars came out over the darkening fields.

She caught his eyes on her, and she pushed aside her glass. "I'm a little tired," she said. "I think I'll go up to bed."

He nodded. "Let me know if there's anything you need."

"All right. Good night."

He stood up when she did, holding her chair for her.

"Good night, Marla." She glanced upward at him from under her thick lashes and saw him watching her with an unreadable expression in his eyes, like the mist rising from Horseshoe Falls. "Well, good night," she murmured again, still not moving away from him. She could feel the heat emanating from his body and remembered how warm she was when he held her close. She sucked in her breath softly when he took her chin in his hand, not daring to open her eyes and look at his face. She felt his breath on her mouth first, and she parted her lips in sweet expectancy. His kiss was gentle, and then he drew away. "Sleep well, Marla," he said softly.

She mounted the stairs slowly without looking back. Once inside her room, she finally let herself relax completely. She took a hot bath and put on one of the silk nightgowns he had bought for her. Slipping into bed she felt tears coming to her eyes. How was she ever going to make it until Winter Carnival? Every minute she was in his presence she could feel herself giving in to him more and more, wanting him more than she had a year ago, if that were possible. It was torture knowing he was enjoying her plight. He was getting just what he wanted—bittersweet revenge.

She squeezed her eyes tightly shut, and a tear rolled down her cheek. Brushing it away, she curled her hand into a fist beside her cheek and let exhaustion claim her.

She was dreaming that he had come to her bedroom and was telling her he wanted her. She reached out and entwined her arms around his neck, feeling the rough sensuality of his hair between her fingers.

She awoke suddenly to gentle pressure on her lips. Her startled eyes flew open to meet amused flinty ones.

"Good morning, *ma petite*," he greeted her with a laugh. "You certainly were sleeping soundly."

Color flooded her face as she realized her arms were indeed around his neck, and she quickly withdrew them, pulling the covers up to her neck. "What are you doing here?" she cried.

"It's time for you to get up. We have to be at work in an hour."

"Work?" she asked, confused.

"Yes, work. Don't tell me you thought you were going to get out of it this easily. Although, if you want, I suppose I could make a proper housewife out of you. While I'm gone today you could scrub a couple of floors, cook the meals, and do some laundry."

"I'll go to work," she murmured distastefully.

"I thought so," Brent said, grinning. "Here, put on your robe and come down for some coffee."

Marla groaned and burrowed into the covers, curling up into a ball. Laughing, Brent gave her a hearty smack on her behind and tossed the robe on the bed. "Five minutes, my dear, and then I'm coming back up here and dragging you out of bed. And that's a promise."

As soon as he was gone, she slipped hurriedly out from under the covers and pulled on the robe. She hadn't expected him to make her go to the office today, though she should have known he would. After all, one of the reasons he'd married her was to assure a smooth transition of power in the company. Shivering, she went downstairs to the kitchen, where the smell of coffee quickened her hunger. Brent was sitting at the table, reading the morning newspaper. He got up and poured her a cup of coffee, then said, "Would you like some breakfast? Henri made French toast."

"I'll get it," she offered, and he sat down again. She filled a plate for each of them and returned to the table. He put aside his paper and made small talk while they ate, mentioning details he wanted to investigate at work that day. Finally, he glanced at his watch. "I'd better shave and get ready."

Marla finished her coffee, then went upstairs and put on a navy blue jersey dress that belted at the waist. With a white cardigan sweater and navy heels she looked slender and attractive. She brushed her hair back from her face and caught it at the nape of her neck with a clip, then freed a few tendrils to frame her face. She hurried downstairs.

Brent was waiting for her in the foyer, and he smiled appreciatively when he saw her. "Very nice," he said in a low voice.

All morning at work, people came up to them to congratulate them and give them their best wishes, and Marla's face was nearly stiff from the constant smiling. Between these interruptions, Brent sent her on one errand after another to gather information for him. He was all cool efficiency and very businesslike, acting like his familiar arrogant self again.

It was with a great deal of surprise that she walked back into what was now Brent's office with a file he'd requested and found Jack standing there.

She greeted Jack warmly, genuinely pleased to see him, and she couldn't help noticing Brent's frown.

"Phillips had a few things he wanted to discuss with you concerning the Syracuse office, Marla," Brent said dryly. "He said he didn't want to disturb us on our honeymoon."

"It's so good to see you, Jack," Marla said. "How long can you stay?"

"I don't know," Jack replied, clearly ill at ease. "I'll leave as soon as I get everything taken care of."

"Well, I hope it's a long stay," Marla said. "Come on. We'll go to my desk, and I'll see what I can do to help you." She started to leave, then as an afterthought turned to Brent. "By the way, here are the files you asked for. Let me know if there's anything else you need."

"I'll be sure to do that," he commented coolly, and she suppressed a smile at the scowl on his face. She was enjoying making Brent feel uncomfortable for a change. After all, he'd banished her to a lonely desk amidst the other workers, a move calculated to show her who was in charge. He had promised her an office of her own as soon as one could be remodeled next to his, but still she resented the temporary exile. At least he had kept his word about her position in the company. He consulted her on nearly everything.

A while later, she was working at her desk with Jack when Brent came by with some correspondence he wanted her to check. "Find out what we did with these accounts in the past, Marla," he said.

"All right," she said, distracted. "I'll take care of it this afternoon."

"Right now, if you don't mind." The ominous tone of his voice made her look up, and she saw the hard coldness in his eyes as they bored into her.

"You're the boss," she said coldly. "And I assume that's an order."

"That's right, my dear," he said in a low tone. "It's an order."

"Then I'll take care of it right now. Excuse me a moment, Jack."

Marla stood up and swept past an angry Brent. She knew full well what he thought of her relationship with Jack, but she also knew he had too much pride to say anything to Jack about it. He would just have to fume while she continued to spend as much time with Jack as she could.

When she had hunted down the correspondence he wanted, she tapped on the door to his office before going in. She would keep this encounter as businesslike as possible. "I believe this is what you wanted," she said, setting the folders down on his desk. "The top one covers the Coolidge account for the past year. If you want anything prior to that, I'll recheck the file." She started to sort through the files, but his hand caught her wrist.

"What are you trying to do, Marla?" he asked with cool anger.

"Just what you ordered me to," she replied tartly, turning her wide blue eyes on him.

"Don't play the innocent." He stood up swiftly and

walked around the desk to her. "Did you ask Phillips to come here?"

"Jack?" she asked with mock surprise. "Of course not. He simply has some things to clear up from the Syracuse office."

"Then make sure there's nothing more going on than business," he warned her. "And be sure you don't prolong it. I want him out of here as soon as possible."

With a cool smile of triumph she turned and started for the door, but his commanding voice halted her. "I have some things to finish this morning. We'll be eating lunch late."

"But I don't want to be rude to our guest," she said in a sweet voice. "I'll take Jack out to lunch at the regular time."

She spun on her heel to leave but stopped short at the door, her heart constricting with pain. Standing in front of her was the woman from her nightmares, the red-haired woman she'd seen Brent with last year. Marla paled and swallowed hard, unable to speak.

"Is Brent in?" the woman asked in a cool voice, obviously mistaking Marla for a secretary.

"Yes," Marla whispered, stunned, moving slowly aside. She watched as the woman breezed past her, a warm smile lighting her face as she spied Brent.

"Brent!" she cried. "I didn't know you were back."

"Sylvia," he said quietly, his eyes on Marla, who was staring at them. "Marla, this is Sylvia Morelle, an old friend of the family and my assistant at Daricom. Sylvia, this is my wife, Marla."

"Your wife?" she cried in surprise, turning around and advancing toward Marla, a speculative smile on her face. "So nice to meet you, Marla," she murmured.

"My pleasure," Marla said quickly. She stood awkwardly, her eyes on the attractive red-haired woman dressed in a clinging green dress. It was easy to see what Brent saw in her. She was a knockout.

"Go ahead back to work, Marla," Brent said in a cool, even tone, dismissing her with a nod. "I'm sure Sylvia has some work from my office at Daricom she wants to discuss with me."

Marla didn't trust herself to reply, so she merely nodded. "It was nice meeting you, Sylvia," she said.

"I'd been looking forward to it," the redhead replied with a calculating smile, and Marla hurried out the door, clenching her fists.

When she returned to her desk, Jack was sitting in thoughtful silence, and he looked up with worried eyes. "Marla, I don't want to cause any trouble between you and Mr. Stevens. If there's going to be a problem for you, I'll leave for Syracuse now."

"No, Jack, don't go," she said. "The problem's between Brent and me. I don't want it to affect our friendship."

He hesitated. "All right. Whatever you say. You know I think of you as a sister."

"Thank you, Jack," she said, smiling with effort. "Now what do you say we go to lunch? I know a great little place."

"What about your husband?"

"He can't make it, so I told him we'd go ahead."

"Okay, but let's finish up this project first."

When Marla got her coat before lunch, Jean was just going into Brent's office, and she shot Marla a harried smile and rolled her eyes. Marla smiled tightly. Apparently Brent was still irritated by her defiance. She was glad she'd ruined his meeting with Sylvia.

The rest of the afternoon sped by. Marla forced herself to smile every time Brent came by her desk, glowering.

She hadn't even realized the office had emptied until she looked up from a discussion with Jack to see Brent looming over her desk.

"It's time to go home, Marla," he said in a low, even voice, his eyes cold and hard.

She stared back at him, feeling her heart begin to beat faster at the implied threat she read on his face. Still staring at Brent, she said, "Shall we call it a day, Jack?"

"I think so," Jack said agreeably, clearly hoping to smooth the ground between Brent and Marla. "We got a lot accomplished this afternoon."

"Have you got a place to stay, Phillips?" Brent asked, his eyes locked with Marla's. "The company suite is vacant right now if you want it."

"Thank you, but no," Jack said. "I've already made arrangements." He cleared his throat awkwardly and added, "I think I'll head back there now. It's been a tiring day." He looked at them again, then picked up his papers and left them there together, like two gladiators prepared to fight to the death.

On the ride home the tension between them was as sharp and icy as the frozen landscape. Marla stared straight ahead, not daring to look at Brent lest her teeth start chattering in fright. She was suddenly unsure of herself and wondered what she would do once they were home. All of her bravado was rapidly evaporating, the closer they drew to the house. It was his fortress, and she had no real place there.

He opened the car door for her, and she walked woodenly beside him as he guided her up the cobblestone walk, his grip on her arm a fierce reminder of his anger.

Inside, the door closed behind them like a cell door slamming. "Go change your clothes. I'll expect you back down here in fifteen minutes."

As she changed into a pair of jeans and a sweater, she heard him come upstairs to his own room. She waited until he left again, then slipped out into the hall and quietly made her way to the stairs.

She stopped when she saw him in the foyer, his back to her. He was reading a letter from the pile Henri had left on the table there, and then, to her surprise, he crumpled it up with an impatient gesture and tossed it into the wastebasket. She backed hastily out of sight just before he turned to look up at the landing, and when she was sure he'd gone into the kitchen, she ventured silently downstairs.

She could hear him opening the refrigerator, making preparations for dinner, and with her heart pounding she stole over to the table and retrieved the letter from the wastebasket. After a hasty, nervous glance toward the kitchen, she read it.

> *Dear Brent,*
> *I called to thank you for the lovely roses and the lunch, but you'd already left Quebec. It was so thoughtful of you to think of me when you had so much on your mind. Naturally I was astounded to learn of your marriage, especially since we'd seen each other so much recently, but I'm sure you had your reasons. I'll look forward to hearing from you when you return.*

Marla paled as she read the letter, and angry tears came to her eyes when she saw the curving signature: *All my love, Syl.*

Roses for Sylvia and violets for Marla. She wondered if Brent kept a reference list of the different tastes of his wife and his mistress. Her stomach lurched as she remembered the time a florist had mistakenly delivered her stepfather's flowers, meant for his latest mistress, to Marla's mother instead. She could still vividly recall the rage and pain in her mother's eyes when she read the card to "My darling Angela." Her mother's name was Jane.

With a bitter twist to her lips, Marla dropped the letter back into the wastebasket. No wonder Brent hadn't wanted her to see it.

Straightening up, she walked to the kitchen, her eyes cold and glittering. He looked up when she came in, but didn't speak, and she set about wordlessly working beside him, fixing a salad while he cooked steaks on the kitchen grill.

When the meat was sizzling, he took out a bottle of wine and poured them each a glass. "No, thank you," she said coldly as he held out the glass.

"Drink it. You'll wish you had later." He pushed the glass into her hand, then turned back to the steaks.

Henri had left two baked potatoes warming in the oven, and Marla put them on plates, then dished out the salad. Brent carried the steaks to the table and they sat down, Brent politely holding out her chair as always. But they ate in tense silence, and Marla found it difficult to swallow her wine. She toyed with her food, feeling his gaze on her throughout the meal. Finally, she pushed aside her plate. He reached over to refill her wine glass, but she said, "No. I don't want any more. I'm really tired. I think I'll go now." She stood up quickly, and he stood too as she left the room. Upstairs, she sagged against the door in her bedroom, relieved he hadn't stopped her.

She washed her face, changed into her nightgown, and was just about to turn back the covers when the door connecting their rooms burst open. She stood mutely, too startled to speak, as Brent advanced into the room, his gray eyes seeming darker than ever as they raked over her.

"Ready for bed, my dear wife?" he asked coldly.

"You've been drinking," she accused him, and he laughed, sending chills down her spine.

"Apparently I haven't been drinking enough, because I can't erase your flagrant disregard of our agreement from my mind."

"What are you talking about?"

She was unable to move as he walked slowly toward her, his eyes never leaving hers. "Your tryst with Phillips today, my dear. What else would I be talking about?"

His voice was low and calm, belying a white-hot fury.

She backed up instinctively and found her back pressed against the bedpost. Further retreat was impossible. When he had drawn within inches of her, she closed her eyes tightly, half expecting him to strike her. Instead she felt his hands clamp down on her shoulders, and she shuddered as his fingers dug into her cruelly. A gasping sob tore from her throat as she felt his breath fan her cheek before he imprisoned her mouth against his own. His lips were commanding, and she opened her mouth to him, but refused to respond as he continued to kiss her. Perhaps her lack of response would cool his anger. But he demanded more of her. When she was rendered nearly senseless by his kiss, he moved his lips to her shoulder, pushing aside her nightgown and wreaking havoc with her will as he nibbled at the tender flesh in the hollow of her collarbone.

"Please," she whispered desperately, but he laughed softly and moved his marauding lips to her neck, sending shivers of pleasure through her. Paralyzed by fright and a spreading pleasure, she could only pant her protests as he continued his play. With a quick, savage gesture, he pulled her nightgown to the waist, and she gasped in alarm, raising her arms to push him away. But he easily imprisoned her wrists in one hand and went back to his intimate exploration of her body with his lips and tongue.

In moments he had her writhing beneath his touch, fire licking her skin as his kisses moved lower.

"Please don't." she cried out, panic-stricken, nearly lost to his superior manipulation of her senses.

"Why not?" he demanded roughly. "You knew the terms, and you chose to violate them. You're only getting what you bargained for."

"No," she begged helplessly. "I didn't break our agreement. I swear it."

"Do you find my kisses so repugnant that you'd lie to avoid them?" he asked hoarsely, his free hand slipping to her waist and pressing her against him. "Don't lie anymore. Your body's betraying you. Shall I show you how much you really want me?"

"No," she cried out in a ragged voice. "Please stop. I didn't do anything with Jack. We just had lunch. I'm not lying."

Her eyes had filled with tears at his accusation, and they threatened to spill over. Wanting to spare herself that humiliation, she tried frantically to free her hand to brush them away, but he wouldn't allow her even that. She stood before him, crying silently, lowering her head to avoid his piercing gaze.

He jerked her chin up, but her lashes lay damply against her pale cheek, and the sight of her terror seemed to sober him somewhat. "Nothing happened between you today?" he demanded harshly, and she shook her head vehemently.

Slowly he released her hands and backed away. "I don't know why I should believe you," he said in a low voice, "but I don't think you're lying this time." She crossed her arms over her naked breasts and watched him from under lowered lashes as he slowly withdrew from her.

"Good night, Marla," he said at the door. "Take care that you don't give me reason to suspect you again. That's a warning."

Then he was gone. Marla slid down the bedpost to the floor, clutching her nightgown to her, her body wracked with silent sobs. He had nearly taken her to bed this night, and only her protests of innocence had saved her. What frightened her most of all was how easily he seduced her, even when she was terrified and angry. And worst of all, he knew it.

He had been cold and cruel in his arousal of her tonight, inflicting his lovemaking on her as a punishment. There was no trace of the tender lover she'd once known. Maybe he had never really existed.

Shaking uncontrollably, Marla crawled into bed and pulled the covers up tightly to her chin, wincing every time she thought she heard a sound from the other room. She couldn't help wondering what was on his mind now. Was he still angry over her attentions to Jack that afternoon, or had his thoughts returned to Sylvia Morelle?

CHAPTER
Six

THEY WERE INVITED to a party that weekend given by two of Brent's closest friends. It was intended to celebrate their marriage, but to Marla the party was a hollow mockery. Nevertheless, Brent made it clear he expected her to accompany him.

"The party is in honor of our marriage," he said coldly, "although I'm sure that fact amuses you, considering our current circumstances."

She shrugged, and he caught her hair, holding her head immobile as he stared down into her blue eyes. "But then maybe you threw a party each time you took a new lover," he said broodingly.

"I'll go with you," she said in a low voice. "Please let me go."

He released her as though suddenly aware of his vicious hold on her, and she sank gratefully into a chair. More and more he seemed determined to punish her for what she'd led him to believe was her scarlet past.

That Friday night they drove in silence to a small club

where the party was being given. Jack had left for Syracuse again, but there was more paperwork to do, and Marla knew he'd be returning. She wasn't sure if she should look forward to seeing him again or not, especially given Brent's violent reaction.

Brent solicitously took her wrap when they entered the reception room, then he guided her over to their host and hostess.

"Marla, these are my dear friends, Miriam and Ben Marquette," he said, a smile touching his eyes as he presented her to them.

Marla looked into a face that seemed full of kindness and felt immediately drawn to the middle-aged woman warmly taking her hand.

"We've so looked forward to meeting you, Marla," Miriam said with a throaty laugh. "Brent's an old friend of ours, and we've been eagerly waiting to meet the woman special enough to lead him to the altar."

"Marla had to take care of business in Syracuse," Brent said smoothly. "I'm afraid our plans were delayed somewhat."

"A whole year," Ben protested, his florid face as full of merriment as his wife's. "I don't see how you waited so long for her, Brent. She's lovely. So happy to meet you, Marla."

Marla returned their greetings, then stood stiffly beside them, joining Brent in meeting the other guests.

Her smile was frozen on her face and she was longing for the ordeal to be over, when the door swung open again and Marla stared at the advancing figure, her eyes wide with shock.

It was Sylvia Morelle again! What was she doing here?

She hardly felt Brent's hand on her arm as he said, "Marla, you remember Sylvia?"

"Of course," Marla said stiffly, taking in the woman's wide green eyes, curled hair, and clinging orange dress.

She made a striking figure, and Marla suddenly wished she could flee the club and never see her again.

"I've heard so much about you," Sylvia said coolly, her eyes taking in the black cocktail dress that Marla wore.

"Don't believe half of it," Marla breathed tightly.

A thick tension hung between them until Sylvia moved away, calling gaily to some friends across the room. "Sylvia's father and my father were friends for many years," Brent said, watching Marla closely. "Sylvia works in the office at Daricom."

Marla turned on him with narrowing eyes and hissed, "I'm sure she's a valuable asset."

"What's this, my dear?" Brent asked with an amused smile. "Could you possibly be jealous?"

"Why should I be?" she demanded in a whisper. "You married me, not her. Now, if you'll excuse me a moment, I'm going to get a drink." Her head held high, she pulled away from him and headed for the bar. No, she wasn't jealous. After all, Brent could have married Sylvia, and he hadn't. But what he *had* done was to meet her secretly while he was engaged to Marla the year before. And now he and Sylvia would take up where they had left off.

She rejoined Brent in the receiving line with a Scotch and soda, ignoring his questioning gaze. Another couple entered the room, and Marla turned her full attention to them, smiling brightly as she was introduced.

When it seemed that the last guests had arrived, Miriam turned to Marla and said, "I hope this isn't all frightfully boring to you. Most everyone here is connected with Brent's company."

"Not at all," Marla said, smiling. "I'm interested in everything about Brent."

"You sound like a loving young bride," Miriam said wistfully.

"I'm afraid not," Marla said, wrinkling her nose. "It's just good business practice to know everything there is to know about your partner, It can save you from nasty surprises years later." She tipped her glass at Miriam, who broke into peals of laughter as Marla headed for a refill at the bar.

Studiously avoiding Brent, Marla mingled with the guests, making small talk, laughing at their jokes, and refilling her glass frequently. Turning from a group of men she had just finished discussing electronics with, she abruptly ran into Sylvia and Brent.

"Excuse me," Marla said coolly. "I was just on my way to the bar."

"You've made enough trips to the bar tonight," Brent said in a low whisper, and Marla noticed Sylvia's curious eyes on her.

"I've just been enjoying myself, dear," Marla responded. "Isn't that what you wanted?"

"Getting yourself drunk isn't what I had in mind," Brent drawled in a dangerously low voice. "I suggest you make that your last drink."

"And I suggest you mind your own business," Marla said with a fixed smile on her face.

She saw the muscles of his jaw tighten imperceptively, and a cold light glittered in his dark eyes. "I'll reckon with you later," he muttered softly, and then he strode away, leaving Sylvia standing there watching Marla.

"My, he does have a temper, doesn't he?" Sylvia commented coolly.

"It's just that I bring out the worst in him," Marla replied quickly.

"I can see that," Sylvia said. "It was a short honeymoon, Mrs. Stevens."

Marla narrowed her eyes. "And what makes you think it's over?"

Sylvia laughed shortly. "I know Brent, Mrs. Stevens. And, believe me, the way he was looking at you doesn't mean candlelight and wine. I don't know how you lured him into marrying you, but something's gone sour rather early in the marriage, I'd say."

"And do you plan on stepping in?" Marla asked bluntly.

Sylvia shrugged. "I won't pretend I wouldn't have married him if he'd asked. And from the look of things, it may not be too late."

"That certainly speaks well of your moral standards," Marla said sarcastically.

"I go after what I want," Sylvia said. "Marriage or no marriage."

"So does Brent," Marla countered. "If he wanted you, nothing would stand in his way."

Sylvia's eyes shot sparks at Marla. "Believe me, Mrs. Stevens, if Brent doesn't love you, I'm going to get him, sooner or later."

"I admire your honesty," Marla said coldly, keeping her voice steady with effort. "I also applaud your devotion to lost causes." She watched Sylvia flush in anger, but before the redhead could retort, Miriam came up to them.

"I hate to drag Marla away, Sylvia," she said, "but there are so many things I want to discuss with her."

"Of course," Sylvia said curtly. "I was planning to visit with Brent anyway."

She stalked away, and Marla turned to Miriam. "Thanks for the rescue," she said gratefully. "Another minute and I might have hit her. Another drink and I'm sure I would have."

"You're a delight, Marla," Miriam laughed, running her hand through her salt and pepper hair. "Brent certainly showed some intelligence when he married you."

Marla flushed under the compliment, thinking that Miriam would be flabbergasted if she knew the true circumstances of their marriage. She glanced across the room at Sylvia and clenched her lips when she caught Sylvia's eye as the redhead latched onto Brent's arm.

Miriam followed Marla's gaze. "She doesn't give up easily."

"Was Brent close to her?" Marla asked suddenly, half

fearing the answer she might receive.

Miriam considered before she spoke. "They were thrown together often. I imagine you know their fathers were good friends." Marla nodded, and Miriam continued. "Sylvia's father is a wealthy jeweler. For a while we all thought Sylvia and Brent would be married someday, but apparently it never developed into that kind of relationship. You came along, Marla, and Brent fell head over heels, as they say."

Marla smiled wryly. If Brent had loved her once, and she doubted it, he certainly didn't love her now. With Sylvia setting her sights on him, this farcical marriage might end sooner than even Marla had anticipated. But if Sylvia had her way, that end would be a humiliating one. Marla could imagine the gossips spreading the word that Brent had dumped her for Sylvia.

"You seem pensive, dear," Miriam said with concern. "Is everything all right?"

"I'm fine," Marla said, forcing a smile. "Just fine."

"There you girls are," a big voice boomed, and Ben came up behind them. "Come along now. I want Marla to meet some more people." Miriam fell into step with him, and Marla followed after a hasty look over her shoulder at Brent. He was leaning casually against the windowsill, Sylvia standing close beside him, laughing huskily at something he said. He turned his head and saw Marla watching him, and for a moment their eyes locked. Then Marla turned and hurried after Ben and Miriam.

By the time Brent and Marla left the party it was quite late, and she was feeling the effects of the numerous drinks she'd consumed during the evening. He said nothing as he helped her on with her coat and took her arm in his firm grip. They said good night to Ben and Miriam at the door and thanked them for the party. As they started down the steps, Miriam gave Marla a reassuring wink and smile, and Marla smiled gratefully back. Sylvia had waited to leave until the last of the partygoers had exited, and had said good night to Brent with smiling sweetness, giving Marla a cool glance.

They arrived at the farmhouse, and Marla hurried upstairs as soon as they entered the foyer, while Brent was hanging up their coats. Her head felt light from the drinks and her footsteps were unsteady. She had no wish for a confrontation with Brent.

But he had other ideas, as she soon discovered. Returning from the bathroom, she stopped abruptly when she saw him in the doorway, the light behind him casting ominous shadows.

"What are you doing here?" she whispered uncertainly.

"I came to help you get ready for bed," he said quietly. "I'm sure your faculties are somewhat impaired after the amount of alcohol you indulged in tonight."

"I'm quite fine," she snapped, starting purposefully across the room. "I don't need any help."

She started to turn down her covers, conscious of his eyes on her the whole time. She turned to go to the closet for her nightgown, and whether it was the drinks or the effect of his presence she wasn't sure, but her heel caught in the rug and she stumbled. Instantly he was beside her, his arm locked around her waist.

"I'm all right," she protested, but her voice carried no conviction, and his answer was to sweep her up and deposit her on the bed. Before she could recover sufficiently to move away he was rolling her onto her stomach and unfastening her dress. She tried to rise, but a firm hand on the small of her back kept her prone. He turned her over on her back then and began pulling the dress from her shoulders, still without a word.

"Will you leave me alone?" she cried plaintively.

But he ignored her, pulling her into a sitting position until the dress was down to her waist, then laying her back and pulling it over her hips. He tossed the dress over a chair and lowered her slip straps.

She grabbed for his hands to stop him, but he pushed hers aside and pulled the slip all the way off. She froze as his eyes traveled over her body. Unconsciously she raised her hands to cover her lacy bra, and a wry smile flitted across his handsome features.

He sauntered over to her closet and came back with her nightgown, then stood beside the bed, staring down at her. She swallowed hard as he sat down on the bed again and flinched when he suddenly caught her hands, imprisoning them in one of his. Slowly he reached out, and she shut her eyes as she felt his free hand lightly touch the lace. Then the last piece of clothing on her torso came off. She knew he was looking at her, and she shivered slightly, wondering what he would do next.

It seemed an interminable wait, and then she felt the nightgown drop onto her. A second later he released her hands. She opened her eyes in surprise as he got up from the bed. Clutching the nightgown to her, she could only stare at him as he walked to the door, where he turned and surveyed her sardonically. "Good night, my dear," he said. "Sleep well."

A minute later she heard him opening drawers in his own room, and she knew he was getting ready for bed. Hurriedly she slipped the nightgown over her head, curled down under the covers, and allowed herself to relax slowly.

She slept deeply from the effects of the drinks and woke groggily the next day to an annoying tickle on her face. She murmured her protests and lazily rubbed her nose, but the annoyance continued. Slowly she opened her eyes, blinking hard in the light that streamed through her window. Brent was tracing a line down her nose and then over her lips. His gentle touch was deeply sensuous, and she felt a warmth spreading throughout her body. Sleepily she looked up into his face and saw amusement etched on his hard features.

observed. "How do you feel?"

She moved to sit up, then sank back down as her head began throbbing. "Just fine," she lied, and he laughed heartily.

"You don't sound very convincing," he informed her. "Why don't you get up and show me just how good you feel?"

"What time is it?" she asked, ignoring his challenge.

"Almost noon. Now hurry up. We're due at Ben and Miriam's in an hour."

"What?" she asked in confusion.

"You were so charming last night that they insisted we come over for lunch today. And cocktails," he added with a grin. "They're entertaining some students who are in town for a ceremony."

"Ceremony?" she repeated, curious in spite of her throbbing head.

"That's right. Ben gave me my start in business, in case you didn't know. He's dedicated to helping young men get going in the business world. These students have won fellowships for graduate studies, fellowships funded in part by Ben."

"And he invited us?"

"In your brief encounter with Ben and Miriam last night you managed to make quite an impression," he said dryly. "Now get dressed or I'll have to help you. Henri's making us some coffee."

Her stomach lurched alarmingly at the mention of food, but he was already out the door. Gingerly she pushed back the covers and sat up. Her head was pounding and her mouth dry, but she managed to stagger to the dresser to find something to wear.

When she emerged downstairs fifteen minutes later in a deep blue suit, Brent was sitting at the table with a cup of coffee. "Here she is, Henri," he said with a grin. "Now, what do you suppose she'd like this morning?"

Marla glared at him as she sank into the chair opposite

his, and Henri bustled about at the sink. "Monsieur is teasing you, madame," the little man called over his shoulder. "I have just the remedy for your malady."

He carried a tall glass to the table and set it before her. "This is my secret medicine," he said proudly. "It has worked wonders in my family for years."

Marla stared at the glass of thick liquid, an unappetizing beige color, and said, "Really, Henri, I appreciate this, but I don't think I could get anything down right now."

"Try, madame," he insisted. "I'm sure this will help."

"You'd better drink up, Marla," Brent warned teasingly, "or I'll have to administer the medicine myself."

She stared at the glass balefully. "What's in this, anyway?"

"Just what you need," Henri assured her. "There is milk and a little orange juice, a small amount of cream, a raw egg, and just a touch of brandy."

Marla paled and raised her fist to her mouth. "Oh, I couldn't."

"But, I assure you you'll feel much better when you drink it," Henri protested, and he had such a hurt look on his face that Marla decided to take a sip just to appease him.

To her surprise, it tasted pretty good, and she took another tentative sip as Henri beamed.

Steeling herself, she drank the rest of the concoction, then smiled weakly at Henri. "Thank you," she murmured.

"You will see," he said convincingly. "You'll feel just fine."

She actually did feel better ten minutes later when Brent finished his coffee. He looked her over and pronounced her much improved in appearance. "Shall we go?"

She nodded and followed him to the foyer. "Have a good time," Henri called after them. "Do you want me to leave something for dinner tonight?"

"No, Henri," Brent said. "We'll fix something ourselves, thanks."

Ben and Miriam lived in a stylish town house in Quebec City, and they greeted Brent and Marla warmly at the door. "How are you, dear?" Miriam inquired as they came in.

"I'm fine," Marla said, actually feeling much better after Henri's remedy.

They commented briefly about the upcoming Christmas holidays, then went into the dining room where Ben and Miriam introduced them to two young men. Jeff and Marcel were recent graduates of the University of Toronto. The foundation that Ben headed had recently awarded them fellowships to continue their studies, and Ben wanted to entertain them while they were in town for the presentation.

A maid brought in a tray of Bloody Marys, and Marla looked at Brent, hesitating. But he smiled and said, "Go ahead. Henri's tonic is guaranteed."

She joined the rest in a toast to the two young men and then listened as they told tales of their school days.

When lunch was served, Marla was seated next to Marcel and across from Brent, who regarded her with amusement as eggs Benedict were set in front of her.

"Marla, you haven't told us about your background," Miriam said at one point. "Do you have family in Quebec?"

"No," Marla replied in a low voice. "My parents aren't living."

"I'm so sorry, dear. You're so young. As I recall, your father founded Stanford Electronics, didn't he?"

"Yes. After his death my stepfather ran it and then my stepbrother and myself."

"Well, you have capable hands helping you to run the business now," Miriam said. "Brent's the best there is."

"Isn't he though?" Marla asked softly, regarding him with cool eyes.

"Actually, Marla is quite capable of running the business without any assistance from me," Brent said, putting down his glass. Marla looked at him in surprise. "She's a woman of many talents." He smiled coolly, his eyes riveted on her and she flushed in embarrassment, knowing he was alluding to her supposed lovers.

"Do you speak French, Madame Stevens?" Marcel asked, and Marla turned her attention to him, smiling as she shook her head. "What a pity," he said.

"Brent has been teaching me though," Marla added, and the boy's eyes lit up.

He began speaking French, and Marla laughingly asked him to slow down. Patiently he began again, and she was able to understand some of what he said. Soon they were laughing together over her mispronunciation, and she was asking him to name the items on the table in French. She glanced up, her eyes glowing in amusement, and found Brent's dark eyes watching her from under heavy lids. He was leaning back in his chair, his arms crossed over his chest, the glass held tightly in one hand. She knew she was irritating him by flirting with the young French Canadian, but she didn't care. She quickly turned her attention back to Marcel.

When they had finished lunch and all sat sipping brandy, Marcel and Jeff were drawn into a friendly argument about the French and Italian schools of fencing. Each considered himself superior to his companion, and the bantering was noisy but good-natured.

"Perhaps we can settle this argument to both of your satisfactions," Ben interjected, a twinkle in his eyes as he surveyed the animated faces at the table. "I've always been a great fan of fencing as a means of staying fit. If you'll step into the drawing room, you'll find ample space to try out my foils."

The boys eagerly agreed to the offer, and Ben led them to the next room. "Let's go watch," Miriam suggested to Marla and Brent. "I think you'll enjoy the entertainment, unplanned as it is."

Brent held Miriam's chair for her, then quickly caught up with Marla, who had started for the other room on her own. He caught her arm, and when Miriam was beside them he took her arm as well. "Ladies," he said with a mock bow as they reached the doorway, and Marla noted that his grip on her arm was uncomfortably strong.

While the two young men prepared for a demonstration in the center of the large room, Ben arranged chairs against the far wall for the spectators.

Finally the boys were ready, Marcel armed with his French foil and Jeff with an Italian one. They faced their audience first, their masks held in their left hands. In unison they brought their foils straight up in the air, the guard opposite the mouth, and saluted sharply, bringing the foils quickly toward the ground. Turning to each other, they repeated the salute, then donned their masks.

The boys were inexperienced but enthusiastic, gamboling like kittens at a picnic, and Ben and Miriam laughed at their energetic play. When they had at last tired themselves out, they collapsed laughing. "We're only amateurs," Jeff said, grinning and panting. "I think we overestimated ourselves."

"It was a fine display," Ben said generously, smiling. "We all enjoyed it." Turning to Marla, he added, "Have you ever fenced? Maybe you'd like to take on one of our guests."

"I used to enjoy it quite a bit when I was in school," Marla replied, "but I think our friends are tired out."

"Then I have the perfect solution," Ben said, a gleam in his eye. "Brent will fence with you."

Marla stared open-mouthed at Brent, who was looking at Ben with something akin to stupefaction.

"You used to fence some, didn't you, Brent?" Ben egged him on.

"It's been some time," Brent mumbled, clearly uncomfortable.

"You're not afraid of being beaten by your wife, are

you?" Ben demanded, holding back his laughter. Miriam joined in with the two boys, urging Brent and Marla to take the floor.

Reluctantly, Brent gave in to their cajoling, a frown creasing his face as he took the mask offered by Jeff and then the foil that Ben produced. "Do you prefer a French foil?" Ben asked Marla, and she nodded, suppressing a smile. She had once been a pretty good fencer, and she was looking forward to meeting Brent. It would be great fun if she could beat him in this.

As they stood close together, each adjusting the handles, Brent muttered, "Let's make this quick. I don't fancy being on display."

"Are you afraid of a challenge?" Marla whispered in a teasing voice. "Or do you think you might lose?"

"Quite the confident opponent, aren't you, *ma petite?*" he growled in a low voice the others couldn't hear. "Shall we make it five hits?"

"That's agreeable with me," she said, grinning. *"Bonne chance."*

His only reply was a grim look, and she turned away, giddy with delight at the opportunity to pay him back for his relentless teasing this morning. They saluted their audience, who laughed and clapped and called out encouragement; then they faced each other. Brent's eyes were fixed on her as they saluted, then donned their masks.

They crossed foils, then began. Marla was quick to leap to the offense. She passed her blade beneath his and lunged for the attack, but he parried, feinted, and answered her with a riposte. He swiftly brought his blade over hers, and in a split second she found his blade touching her firmly just above the waist. Stunned by his quickness and expertise, she murmured, "touché," to acknowledge the hit, an embarrassed blush flooding her face.

She tried harder after that, but he frustrated her every

effort. Lunge after lunge by Brent sent her retreating backward, and when she was off balance, he made a straight thrust to her midsection, and she was forced to mumble "touché" again.

He made four quick hits in succession, leaving her breathless and humiliated by the way he was dispatching her. Fencing seemed effortless for him, and she realized she was greatly outmatched.

Their blades were engaged again when he spoke softly; "If you're not feeling well, we could quit now."

She knew he was giving her a way out, a means of saving face in front of everyone, but she held her head up defiantly, her eyes shooting fire. "I'm not a quitter," she murmured in a low voice. "If you win, it will be fair and square."

She couldn't read his expression through his mask and wondered if he was amused by her pathetic display of bravado. Gritting her teeth, she concentrated on parrying his attack. He crossed foils on her right side, then, without changing the position of his hand, moved rapidly to the left, then back to the right. Marla felt helpless and trapped by his speed and agility, and in sheer frustration she lunged foolishly. Her form was bad, and she was way off balance. Her blade missed him completely and, to her complete embarrassment, she dropped her foil. She stared at him as he removed his mask. She was totally unnerved by the match and expected to find him gloating. But he wasn't smiling. He was watching her, apparently waiting for a sign of her frustration. She was determined to give him none. She stood straight and proud and waited for the hit. But instead he lowered his blade slowly. "I believe the match is yours," she acknowledged quietly.

"Then I'm claiming the spoils of victory," he said softly, and she stared at him in wide-eyed wonder as he advanced slowly to her, stopping just inches away. He removed her mask, and as he tilted her chin up she expelled her breath in a ragged sigh. Then his lips captured hers with the same expertise he'd just displayed in their match. But this was a match of a different sort, and she closed her eyes, giving in to the throbbing of her heart as his arms held her close to him.

When the kiss ended, cheering broke out from the others, and they both realized with surprise that they weren't alone. They separated slowly, and Brent bowed to the spectators.

"You're as good as ever," Ben laughed, coming forward to clap him on the back. "I hope you don't mind being put on the spot like that."

"The prize was well worth it," Brent said solemnly, looking at Marla, and she flushed becomingly as the others laughed again.

CHAPTER
Seven

When Marla awoke the next morning, she dressed quickly and went downstairs, where she found Henri pouring coffee. Brent wasn't around, and Henri, catching her glance, said, "Monsieur went to church this morning, madame. He said you were tired and he didn't wish to disturb you. Would you like some breakfast now?"

"No, thank you," she answered. "I think I'll just have some coffee." She settled down at the table while Henri fixed something in the kitchen.

When Marla and Brent had returned the previous night after a long day with Ben, Miriam, and their guests, they had quietly made a steak dinner and then Marla had excused herself to retire early, feigning weariness. Neither had mentioned the fencing match.

"Henri?" Marla began tentatively, and the little man turned from the stove deferentially.

"Yes, madame," he said politely.

"I guess you've been with Mr. Stevens quite some time," she said.

"Oh, yes indeed, madame. Quite some time."

"And I suppose during all that time Mr. Stevens has known a great many women. I mean, being a bachelor and everything." She was staring down into her coffee in embarrassment, wondering how she had the nerve to press him for information, and more important, why.

The little man cleared his throat nervously. "Monsieur has had his share of lady friends, if that's what you mean."

"But surely he's had them here to the house, weekend guests or something of the sort." Her voice trailed off in discomfort.

"Oh, no, madame," Henri said quickly. "I couldn't presume to know the nature of monsieur's relationships outside this house, but he has never entertained here. I think he prefers to keep this as a private place." Marla searched his face but saw only open honesty in Henri's eyes. Yet, it seemed incomprehensible to her that Brent hadn't brought any of his lady friends here. Perhaps it was on evenings when Henri was out.

"You must be right about his feelings concerning his home," she murmured quickly, trying to smile. "I think I'll take a walk now, if you'll excuse me, Henri." He nodded politely as she went to get her coat.

She spent about an hour walking around the grounds, stopping often to admire the thick snow on the evergreens. The sheer silence of the crisp air was utterly peaceful. She was standing under a fir tree looking out over a field, watching a bird wheedle high in the sky when she heard footsteps crunching in the snow. She whirled around and found herself face to face with Brent, his eyes narrowed as he looked down at her.

They stared at each other wordlessly, and then he said, "When Henri told me you'd gone walking, my first thought was that you'd left."

She tilted her head back defiantly. "I told you I'd keep my end of the agreement. As long as you're fair, I'll be the same."

He nodded. "I should have known that. You certainly showed your spirit in fencing yesterday.

"I don't know why you say that," she said shortly. "I must have looked pretty silly."

"Some people would have dissolved into tears or made excuses," he said quietly, reaching out to touch a tendril of her hair. "But you did neither. I admire that."

She didn't know what to say, and he finally broke the mood by dropping his hand to her waist and starting back toward the house with her beside him.

Marla kept busy at work the next day. Jack had returned to town and, despite Brent's glowering gazes, Marla worked with him all day. She was stopped in her tracks later that morning, though, when she entered Brent's office after a perfunctory knock and found Sylvia bending over him at his desk.

He looked up and frowned. "Yes?"

"I'm sorry to bother you," Marla said coldly, feeling close to tears despite her outward composure. Sylvia was watching her with catlike satisfaction. Marla's eyes narrowed. "I just wanted to tell you I finished the Sloane project," she said, "and I'll be eating lunch with Jack." She met Sylvia's gaze.

Brent's jaw tightened. "I'd made reservations for you to eat with Sylvia and me today," he said in a low voice.

"I'm sorry I can't make it," Marla said quickly. "But, after all, Christmas is almost here, and I haven't shopped for your present yet. And I do so want to make it something special." Smiling tartly, she turned and left the office, hearing Brent expel his breath in an angry hiss behind her.

But she derived little satisfaction from her lunch with Jack, and she found it impossible to confide in him. Seemingly against her will, everything had changed. Jack seemed to understand something of what she was going through, and he simply nodded when lunch was over and she told him she wanted to take a walk.

She went down a long row of shops, staring in the windows, wondering what to get Brent for Christmas. She thought of getting him liquor or a jacket, but discarded those ideas. They were the type of thing Sylvia would buy for him. She would have to come up with something more original. Then a quaint antique shop caught her eye, and she stopped at the window, fascinated. There, leaning up against a chair, was what she was looking for. It was the perfect gift for Brent. Smiling, she walked inside and made her purchase.

Christmas and the holidays were suddenly upon them. Brent and Marla held an office party the afternoon of Christmas Eve, just before everyone went home early. Marla headed for the main conference room to join the fun, but stopped short at the door. Sylvia was presiding at the punch bowl, her toothy smile full of self-satisfaction. Marla spun angrily on her heel and headed back to her own desk. Jack had already gone home for a few days, saying he'd return during the holidays to do some skiing. When Marla had coolly asked Brent what Sylvia was doing there the day before, he'd informed her he had another company to run and Sylvia was acting as his liaison.

But Marla was determined not to swallow her pride again and have to put up with the red-haired woman.

Half an hour later she was working diligently on some papers when a shadow fell over her desk, and she looked up to see Brent. "Why aren't you at the party?" he asked.

"I have work to do," she snapped.

His hand snaked out and snatched the papers from her desk. "This can wait until after the holidays," he said, looking at her work.

"I prefer to work," she said pointedly, but he came around the desk and stared down at her.

"I'm not putting up with any of your intrigues," he

said. "Now, do you come to the party under your own free will, or do I carry you in? And believe me, I'll do it."

She read the determination in his eyes and stood up slowly, stiffly. She would give in because there were other people around, but she was furious.

It was as bad as she'd imagined it would be. Sylvia insisted on bringing her a glass of punch, and then someone in the crowd called out, "Look, Brent. Your wife is under the mistletoe. You know what to do, don't you?"

There were whoops of laughter all around, and Brent walked over to a seething Marla and gave her a quick kiss. "Oh," cried Sylvia. "I guess you've caught me under the mistletoe too."

After a lingering look at Marla, who was glaring at him, Brent gave Sylvia a kiss which lasted a fraction of a second longer than the one he'd given Marla. While everyone whooped with laughter, Marla felt her face burn with humiliation. How dare he flaunt his relationship with Sylvia in front of her. Surely the whole office knew. She walked away miserably.

They were silent on the drive home and all through dinner. When the dishes had been cleared away, Brent suggested they decorate the tree, and Marla followed him soundlessly to the huge living room, where Henri had put up the tree Brent had cut. They worked in silence until Brent broke the tension by holding up a glass ornament and telling her its history, how it was the first one his aunt had ever owned. He did the same with every ornament, and she was surprised and secretly delighted to hear the story behind each one. They were all so special. When they were done he lit candles on the mantel and brought in a bottle of wine and two glasses, then poured them each a drink.

"Merry Christmas, Marla," he said, raising his glass to hers.

"Merry Christmas," she returned, feeling a tug at her

heart. This was everything she had ever wanted, but it gave her no satisfaction, because there was no real love between her and Brent. They were sharing their first Christmas as husband and wife, but it was meaningless. There was nothing to celebrate.

When it was almost midnight, Brent asked if she wanted to go to church with him, and she agreed. They lived a short distance from the simple but elegant building, and she found a comforting peace walking on the hard snow through the quiet countryside. When they were almost there the bells began ringing, and Marla felt an inexplicable longing to hold Brent's hand. But she held back.

The service was beautiful in its simplicity, the candles casting a soft glow throughout the old stone building. When they walked back out into the cold night air, Marla felt inexplicably comforted.

At home Brent fixed them coffee, then suggested they open their presents. She got his from her bedroom and brought it back downstairs. He was standing facing the fire, seemingly lost in thought, and turned only when she came up beside him. "Merry Christmas," she said quietly, handing him the package.

"Merry Christmas, Marla," he answered, handing her a small wrapped box.

She opened hers first and to her delight found a set of oil paints. "I thought you might enjoy them," he said simply.

"Thank you," she whispered. "Now open yours."

He still seemed lost in thought, and as he opened the package there was a different expression in his eyes, one she didn't recognize. He drew out an old hand-drawn map of his farm and the surrounding area and looked at it in wonder for a long moment before turning to her, a warm light in his eyes. "Where did you find this?" he asked, and she thrilled at the appreciation in his voice.

"I found it in a little store in town," she said. "I know

how much you love the land, so I thought you'd like it."

"I love it," he said quietly, setting it down gently and drawing her into his arms. She looked up at him, her heart beating faster. "I was wondering if you'd mind going to visit my aunt tomorrow," he said. "She's not well, and it would mean so much to her. She practically raised me by herself after my parents died."

Marla nodded. "I'd like that," she whispered.

"Good. I know she wants to meet you." His head bent lower, and finally she felt what she hungered for, his lips on hers. It was a gentle, lingering kiss, and then he whispered huskily, "Merry Christmas, *ma petite*."

The next day they took a private boat to Île d'Orléans and the immaculate, white frame home of Madame Irene du Bois, Brent's aunt. Marla was apprehensive at first, but as soon as they knocked on the door and she heard a tiny, warm voice calling for them to come in, her fears melted away. The short, thin woman embraced Marla enthusiastically, leaving no doubt that she was quite welcome. But Madame du Bois looked tired, and Marla insisted on helping her and Brent in the kitchen. After a pleasant dinner, during which Brent and his aunt recalled many pleasant memories, Marla helped clear the table and wash the dishes.

They sat in front of the fireplace that evening with their coffee, but Madame du Bois retired early, explaining she was under a doctor's orders to rest. Marla offered to help her to her room, and the old woman clutched her hand gratefully. Once there, she sank down on the bed wearily and patted Marla's hand. "So tell me, my dear, how do you like life with Brent?" she asked.

Taken off guard, Marla could only reply, "Why, I don't know. I suppose I'd call it overwhelming."

Madame du Bois laughed. "Now don't let him fool you. Underneath that gruff exterior is a very generous heart."

Marla avoided the woman's eyes, and Madame du

Bois asked, "What is it, child? You aren't unhappy, are you?"

"Oh, no," Marla said quickly, eager to reassure the woman. She mustn't reveal the circumstances of their marriage. Already Marla liked the older woman, and she didn't want to see her hurt.

"Do you love him, child?"

Marla's eyes met the woman's older, gray ones. "Yes," she whispered, hoping she sounded convincing.

The woman studied her for a long time, then said softly, "Yes, I think you do."

When Marla rejoined Brent, he invited her to take a short walk before they went to bed, and she accepted. They strolled along the edge of the water in the chill air, and Brent put his arm around her when she shivered slightly. He seemed to feel the need to talk, as though being back home was so compelling that he had to speak. "My father was a fisherman," he said. "Salmon fishing was productive here at one time. But now the water is polluted, and everything has changed."

"How did your parents die?" Marla ventured.

"There was a rough year," Brent said, his voice sounding far away. "My father wasn't making enough money from fishing, so my mother went out with him one morning to help. They thought that together they could do better." He paused, and she glanced at his profile and saw the pain in his eyes. "There was a bad storm, and they couldn't get back home. They both drowned."

"I'm so sorry," Marla whispered, deeply moved.

"My aunt Irene brought me to her home and raised me herself. She wanted something different for me, something other than fishing. Because of her I went into business."

He glanced at Marla and saw her eyes on him. "Come on," he said. "Let's go back. You must be cold."

She had wondered about their sleeping accommodations, but found that their room had two beds. She put on her nightgown first and climbed into one of the beds, and a while later Brent came in and got into the other bed. She wondered what he had been thinking in the other room by the fire, but she pretended to be asleep. She didn't know if he would want to share more of his past with her.

They made the return trip home the next day. Brent was in a mellow mood. They talked little on the drive after leaving the boat, but once he pulled her closer to him, and she rested her head on his shoulder. "My aunt was quite taken with you," he said. "She told me to treat you right or she'd take you away from me, have you move in with her."

Marla laughed in spite of herself. "I liked her from the moment I saw her. She's wonderful."

"I'm afraid her health is much worse," he said in a brooding tone. "I asked her to move closer to us so I'd know she was being taken care of, but she wouldn't hear of it. I can't blame her. It's not easy giving up one's independence."

He seemed lost in thought during the rest of the trip, and Marla didn't speak either, content to rest her head on his shoulder.

The day after they arrived back home, he told her she would have to be the hostess for a holiday party he was giving for his friends. When she protested that she didn't know them well enough, he suggested that Sylvia help her, and Marla bit her lip angrily. "If you insist that I give this party, then I'll give it myself," she said coldly. "I certainly don't need her help." He'd looked at her curiously but said nothing, and Marla made the arrangements without assistance.

But out of spite, she looked up the hotel where Jack was staying to ski and called to invite him as well. Brent walked into the room just as Marla said, "All right, Jack. We'll be looking forward to seeing you at the party." She hung up and turned to find Brent regarding her with cool appraisal. "I see you didn't bother to consult me on the guest list," he said coldly.

"I thought you wanted me to give this party," Marla retorted.

With a black look in her direction, he turned and abruptly left the room.

Marla surveyed the arrangements for the party an hour before the guests were to arrive and was satisfied with the results. The living room was filled with holly, poinsettias, and candles, and soft music played on the stereo. The smell of hot hors d'oeuvres wafted from the kitchen as Henri opened the door to carry in a punch bowl. "Do we have the bar well enough stocked?" Marla asked.

"I'm sure it's more than adequate, madame," Henri assured her. "You've done splendidly."

They had invited thirty people, so Marla had ordered most of the food from a caterer and had it warming in the oven.

Satisfied that everything was in order, she went upstairs to dress, hearing Brent showering in his own bathroom. She put on a red silk party dress with full sleeves. Gathered at the waist, it cascaded into a full skirt that moved gracefully with her. The neck was open in a vee, just to the beginning of the soft swell of her breasts. She looked good in the dress, and she smiled to herself as she brushed her hair. Then, as a final touch, she worked two gold combs into her hair.

Sylvia arrived early, even before Brent had come downstairs, and Marla welcomed her with reserve. "I hope I'm not too early," Sylvia purred. "Did I interrupt anything?" Before Marla could reply, Brent appeared on the stairs, and Sylvia, resplendent in a tight green dress, rushed to greet him and take his arm. "You must show me what you've done with the house," she gushed. She pulled him away, and Marla felt heat rise to her face.

Fortunately other guests began arriving, and Marla turned her attention to them. When Jack came, she took him under her wing and introduced him around. Seeing Sylvia clutching Brent's arm possessively, Marla lifted her chin higher and led Jack to the punch bowl. They were soon joined by Sylvia and Brent.

"You've given such a nice party, Marla," Sylvia enthused. "Brent tells me you made all the arrangements yourself. You should have let me help out. I make divine crab canapés that everyone loves, and I would have let you steal the recipe."

"I'm sure you would," Marla said from between clenched teeth. "But I wouldn't want to make a habit of stealing something that belongs to someone else. Obviously, your habits differ from mine." She smiled sweetly at Sylvia and was rewarded by the woman's gasp of outrage.

"Really, Brent," Sylvia protested. "I've never been treated so rudely."

"I assure you I can be even ruder if I choose," Marla said in an icy voice.

Sylvia stalked angrily away, and Jack excused himself, although Marla detected a slight smile at the corners of his mouth before he turned away. She looked up at Brent to find his dark eyes piercing her. "You're behaving intolerably, Marla," he said with barely suppressed anger. "I suggest you change your attitude. And you might also mingle more with our guests instead of dragging Phillips around like a puppy. Remember, you're my wife now."

"You might keep that in mind yourself," she retorted coldly. "Sylvia is beginning to look like an extra appendage." She spun away before he could answer and sought out a small group talking in the corner. If he insisted on playing this charade of possessive husband while entertaining Sylvia, then she would take every opportunity to flaunt Jack at him.

By the time they said good night to their guests, both Brent and Marla had fixed smiles on their faces and ice in their eyes. Henri hurriedly cleared out the dishes, then retired for the night, leaving Marla to blow out the candles while Brent sipped a brandy by the fireplace.

When he turned to look at her, she detected the cold resolve in his features and steeled herself for his attack. "I see you're as determined as ever to make me appear the fool," he said quietly.

"Make you the fool?" she cried in anger. "If you felt the fool, then I'm glad. Because you've been repaid in kind."

"What are you talking about?" he demanded, striding over to her and catching her shoulders in a viselike grip. Her eyes widened, and she was half afraid he would shake her, but her fury overcame her fear.

"I'm talking about Sylvia, as if you didn't know," she hissed. "From the way she remained glued to you the entire evening, I'm sure everyone knows you're carrying on with her."

His eyes narrowed dangerously, and there was an ominous silence before he spoke. "That's laughable considering your relationship with Phillips, not to mention your colorful past. You have no right criticizing whom I associate with, especially considering your propensity for different beds." The last word was spoken with low, venomous emphasis, and his fingers dug into her shoulders. The color drained from her face and then, in unthinking rage she swung her arm and slapped him as hard as she could. He didn't move, didn't even flinch, and they stood staring at each other before he suddenly shoved her from him. Clutching her arms, she stumbled backward. "You'd better retire for the night," he snarled at her, "before I do something I might regret later."

She backed away, her eyes wavering under his iron gaze. She knew he was holding his temper just barely in check, and that to provoke him further would be to invite disaster. At the doorway she turned and fled up the stairs, her heart pounding, whether in anger or terror she didn't know. "Damn him," she cried into her pillow. He had only gotten what he deserved, yet she was the one suffering. He tormented her with Sylvia's presence at every opportunity, then denied her the same liberty with Jack. He was ruthless and seemingly determined to break her spirit.

The next day at work Brent was especially domineering, ordering her to do one simple task after another that the secretaries could have handled easily, until even Jean rolled her eyes and shook her head. But Marla knew he intended to keep her so busy that she wouldn't be able to spend any time with Jack, and she patiently carried out his orders, always returning to her desk and the chair near Jack when she was done. Then the phone on her desk would ring again, and Brent would summon her to his office for the umpteenth time.

She suppressed a smile when he had to consult her on a large equipment proposal, his brows knitted in concentration. "What do you think of this figure?" he asked, showing her the quoted price.

She leafed through the papers. "I'd take off another two percent. We're facing stiff competition on this one." His grunt of assent meant he approved her judgment, and she went back to her desk with a smug smile.

It was lunchtime when the latest summons came, and Marla walked into his office to find Sylvia sitting next to him at the desk, her dress hiked well above the knees as she leaned close to him, ostensibly to get a closer look at some papers on the desk. Marla stiffened and glared at them. "What did you want?" she asked coldly.

"I want you to go over these papers so Sylvia can take them back to the other office with her. They have to do with Daricom operations, but I thought you should be aware of the situation."

She snatched the papers from his desk and perused them, forcing herself to read them a second time when her anger blinded her to what was written there at first glance. It was all in order, an ordinary proposal for some equipment, and she was sure Brent had called her in just to make sure she saw Sylvia and him together.

"They look fine to me," she said.

"Good. Then maybe you're ready for lunch."

"I'm afraid I've already made arrangements."

"What arrangements?" he demanded in a cold voice.

"I'm eating with Jack. Now, if you'll excuse me, I don't want to keep him waiting."

"Marla." His voice halted her at the door, and she turned slowly to face him. "Cancel your arrangements."

There was a peremptory tone to his voice that made it a clear order, one not to be questioned. She saw the determination in his eyes and swallowed hard. She was almost afraid to continue fighting him, but if she gave in on this, she would have lost even more ground. She would be surrendering her pride. Standing as straight as she could, she glanced at Sylvia's calculating eyes and said, "I'm afraid an employee's time at lunch is her own." Then she left, her hands clenched at her side. She shivered as she remembered the fury clouding his face. She was sure he would make her pay for this, but how she didn't know.

At Marla's insistence, she and Jack took some work with them and spent a long lunch. It was almost two and a half hours later when they returned, and Marla saw Brent glance up at them from beside Jean's desk, where he was going over some correspondence. His eyes narrowed as he watched them, and Marla knew his fury hadn't cooled. Well, she was content to let him simmer a while. Apparently Sylvia had returned to the other office, but Marla couldn't help wondering if she had stayed for lunch with Brent.

He didn't speak to her that evening as they drove home, but she noticed that he was gripping the steering wheel tightly.

He escorted her arrogantly into the house, then dismissed Henri, insisting they would make their own dinner. He got out eggs, cheese, and spices and began making omelets. Marla found the bread and made toast. There was some bacon, so she fried that too.

They ate in silence, and then she poured them coffee. He leaned back, the lean angles of his hard face giving him an angry, dangerous air. He surveyed her in silence, then announced, "Tomorrow morning Phillips will receive notice terminating employment."

Marla looked up in shock, her eyes wide and disbelieving. "You fired him?" she cried.

"He doesn't know it yet, but tomorrow he will."

"But how could you? Jack hasn't done anything."

"I told you I didn't want you keeping company with him, and you chose to ignore my warning. You shouldn't be so surprised."

"But that's not fair! Jack is just a good friend."

"Are you trying to tell me you two haven't had any intimate contact since he arrived here?"

"You should know that without my having to say it," she replied angrily, her face burning.

"Maybe you should have told me sooner," he insisted coldly. "You might have saved his job." He stood up and started for the living room. "I'm going to have a brandy and do some reading. You're free to do as you wish."

She wanted to angrily berate him for his condescending attitude, but she knew that would accomplish nothing. She had to humble herself for Jack's sake, so she tried a different tact. "Brent?" she asked softly.

He turned, and she could read no compromise on his face. "Please don't do this," she pleaded in a soothing voice. "It's not fair to Jack." She paused but could see no change in his expression. His gray eyes raked over her impersonally. She swallowed hard, then added, "This means a lot to me. I'm willing to give up a great deal."

Her voice faltered in the face of his hard smile, which

carried no warmth to his eyes. "Are you trying to prop-osition me with your favors if I relent?"

She looked away from him, feeling color rushing to her face in embarrassment. "If that's what you want," she whispered hoarsely.

His harsh laugh made her want to die. "Do you think you can buy me off the way you do your lovers?" he demanded. When she didn't answer, he took her chin in his iron hand, and she was forced to meet his eyes. "Don't make the mistake of thinking you can win me over with your wiles, *ma petite*," he warned her. "I was well aware of your charms and your deceptions when I married you. What worked with the others won't work with me." He released her suddenly, and she stared at him, misery in her eyes. Biting her lip, she turned away and ran up the stairs. He was demanding too much of her. He wouldn't let her fight him. When she used the only weapon she had against him—Jack—he quickly and efficiently eliminated the weapon. It was all so un-fair. He should have gotten angry at her, not fired Jack. She couldn't live with herself, knowing it was her fault that Jack had lost his job. She had used him in her battle with Brent, and now she was ashamed of herself. This was all her fault.

She lay on the bed trying to think of something to do, but nothing came to mind. There didn't seem to be any way she could get Jack back his job. Brent controlled her every move. Well, if that was the case, then she wasn't going to stay here with Brent. She'd told him she would be fair and honor their agreement as long as he was fair himself. He'd done Jack a grave injustice, and she no longer felt constrained by their agreement. To-morrow she would take her Syracuse bankbook, and when Brent was busy at work, she'd go to the airport and leave Quebec. Then she'd at least have a bargaining position—her return to Quebec for Jack's job. Brent would have to change his mind or lose face, letting everyone know his bride had deserted him.

She was trembling with anger at his unfairness and wished she were on a plane away from Quebec at that very moment.

The next morning she slipped the bankbook from its hiding place in a drawer in her room and put it in her purse, then waited upstairs until it was almost time to leave. "Do you want some coffee?" Brent asked in a conversational voice, as though nothing had happened.

"No, thank you. I'll get some at work."

She checked his schedule when they arrived and noticed he had a meeting that afternoon about an hour before closing. That would be ideal. No doubt he would be late getting back to the office, and she'd already be on her way. He'd think she'd gone home by herself.

Jack wasn't anywhere around, and she assumed bitterly that Brent had sent him packing to Syracuse with severance pay. She was nervous most of the morning but relieved when Brent had to take a client to lunch and she had work to do and couldn't go with them. That would avoid any contact with him before she left. She had to admit she was afraid of seeing him again lest he guess her intentions.

But as she watched him leave late that afternoon, she realized she wouldn't be seeing him for a long time, and a part of her grew numb with pain.

As soon as she was sure he was far enough away, she got her purse and coat and caught a taxi for the airport. First she would find Jack in Syracuse and apologize for what she'd done, then she would contact Brent.

At the airport she bought a ticket for the next departure to Syracuse and sat down to wait. It seemed an interminable delay, but it was only an hour and a half before the departure was announced. Marla stood and picked up her purse, ready to board and put Quebec behind her. She was starting down the concourse with the others when a hand on her arm halted her.

Startled, she turned quickly, and her face drained of color. Brent was looming over her, his face dark with rage.

"What are you doing here?" she cried in a quavering voice.

"You should have been more careful, my dear," said savagely. "I've known about your bankbook for a long time. When you took it this morning, I kept close watch on you."

His grip on her arm tightened, he began guiding her away from the departure gate. "Brent, please," she began, but one look from him effectively silenced her. He was obviously in no mood to be questioned. Marla stumbled obediently alongside him, her thoughts in a jumble. What was he going to do now that he had found her? She didn't dare think about that and bit her lip in confusion.

When they finally drove up to the house, Marla shrank down in the seat as Brent strode around the car and opened the door for her. With ruthless pressure on her arm, he pulled her up the walk into the house. Henri disappeared after a gruff word from Brent, and Marla watched his retreating back with trepidation. Now she was truly alone with Brent.

Henri had made a quiche for them, and Marla helped Brent warm it up along with some crusty bread. She tore up lettuce for a salad, then carried the food to the table.

They ate in silence, and Marla was afraid to look at Brent. He must hate her for running out on him for the second time. Yet he'd said nothing.

He seemed lost in thought as he stared down into his wine glass, and Marla sat woodenly, hardly daring to breathe lest she attract his attention. Finally, he stood up in distraction and went to the cupboard. She watched his every move as he took out a pack of cigarettes and tapped one out. He leaned against the counter as he lit it, then turned to regard her through a haze of blue smoke.

Marla wished he would say something, anything, even shout at her, but he continued to look at her with an unreadable expression.

"Is it all right if I go upstairs now?" she asked softly. "I think I'd like to shower."

He nodded briefly, and she slipped from her chair, her legs wobbly as she hurried away. She shut the door to her room and sighed in relief. It seemed he wasn't going to lecture her tonight after all. For that she was grateful. After what had happened, she didn't think she could stand up under another cruel verbal attack from him.

She showered and put on a nightgown and robe, then sat in a chair by her table and tried to read, but was unable to concentrate. A couple of hours later she felt somewhat more relaxed and put down her book to go to bed. Maybe by morning she would be more composed and could explain why she had tried to leave. She pulled the covers up over her and closed her eyes, wishing sleep would take her quickly tonight.

She must have just drifted off when she was awakened by a light in her room. She blinked and saw that the door between her room and Brent's was open letting light in. And standing in the doorway was Brent, his arms crossed over his chest as he leaned against the frame.

"What is it?" she whispered in a shaky voice.

Easily pushing himself away from the door, he sauntered into her room before he spoke. "Our agreement," he said quietly.

"What about it?"

"You broke it by trying to escape me." He paused, and she felt her heart begin to thump against her ribs. "You know what that means, don't you?"

"Please, Brent," she whispered. "I can't."

"You have to, *ma petite*." His voice contained no warmth, though he'd called her by that pet name. "You knew the price."

He came closer to the bed, and in terror Marla tried to roll to the other side. But Brent was quicker. He caught her arm and dragged her back to him. Then, warding off her flailing arms, he swept her up in his arms and held her close to his chest.

"No, Brent," she cried. "It's not the way you think. I only wanted to apologize to Jack. Then I was going to call you, to tell you I'd come back if you'd give Jack back his job."

"I'm sure no apologies were needed," he said coldly as he carried her through the door to his bedroom. "No doubt he even considered his job a fair enough price for your favors."

He deposited her roughly on his bed, and Marla stared up at him, a film of tears in her eyes. "I've never slept with Jack. You've got to believe me, Brent."

"You're a charming liar and a very convincing one," he said, dropping his body over hers just as she tried to get back up. "But it won't work this time." She opened her mouth to protest again, but his mouth came down on it, hard and demanding. She had a sense of drowning, of being unable to help herself, as his tongue probed her mouth, forcing her to gasp for breath. When he finally left her lips to caress her neck, she tried to twist her head away, but Brent caught her hair with one hand and held her head immobile. His mouth began a slow, sensual exploration of her body as his other hand impatiently ripped away her nightgown. The flimsy material gave easily, and Marla's face burned with humiliation as he stripped her bare.

His hot mouth was pressed against her neck, and she moaned and kicked in terror. He threw one leg over hers to hold them still, and she realized she was powerless against him.

He raised his head to look down into her frantic eyes, and a cold smile touched his lips. "Why fight me, Marla?" he demanded softly. "After all, we're married.

We're only going to do what we've done before and what you did many other times with other men."

"No," she panted, wincing as his hand tightened in her hair. "There were no other men. I swear it."

"Another lie?" he said wearily. "Why is it you'll say anything to save yourself from this?"

"It's the truth," she said, tears beginning to trickle down her face. "I lied to you about the others. There's never been anyone but you."

"Are you trying to tell me you've been to bed only with me?" he scoffed. "No one else?"

She nodded, raising her hand to wipe away her tears, but he caught her wrist. "Look at me," he commanded. Slowly she opened her eyes, flushing scarlet at the mockery in his gazes.

"Go ahead and laugh," she cried. "I'm sure you're enjoying this immensely. You must find it very amusing that I lied myself into this predicament."

Slowly he released her wrist, and then he was wiping her face with a handkerchief. "And why didn't you make this confession earlier?" he demanded sharply, and she heard the skepticism still there. "Why did you lead me to believe that you were promiscuous?"

"I didn't want to marry you," she whispered, her voice breaking. "It seemed the easiest way out, to tell you there were others. I thought you wouldn't ask questions then."

He didn't say anything, and she lowered her eyes, then crossed her arms to hide her nakedness. "So you wanted me to believe you didn't love me, and to avoid marriage you lied about other lovers," he said, and she nodded slowly. "It seems you tried everything to keep from marrying me," he commented dryly.

He was still lying next to her, but now he stood up. "Can I go back to my room?" Marla whispered hopefully.

"I'm afraid not."

"But I told you the truth," she cried. "I thought you believed me."

"Oh, I believe you, *ma petite*," he said in a deep voice. "But you've overlooked one thing."

"What's that?" she murmured in a low whisper.

"You've forgotten the fact that you violated our agreement by trying to leave me, and you haven't paid for that yet." He turned to face her, and she saw that he'd undone his shirt and was slipping it off. She couldn't take her eyes from him as he continued to undress, and she froze where she lay. He intended to go through with this.

When he was undressed, he came to her again, gently pulling her hands away from her nude body. He began to kiss her neck with tender nibbles, then moved to her collarbone, exploring the hollow there with his tongue. She felt a familiar fire lick through her veins and moaned. His mouth moved lower, his hands stroking her legs. "Please, Brent," she pleaded softly, but there was a catch to her voice. He raised his head to look into her eyes, and a wry smile turned up the corners of his mouth as he read her surrender there. "Tonight, *ma petite*," he whispered hoarsely, "your husband is going to make love to you."

As his mouth returned to its play, she gave in to the heady smell of musk and tobacco that clung to him. Groaning, she twined her arms around his neck.

To give in to him like this was to insure herself bitter heartache, she thought as if from a distance. But she was powerless to save herself from that pain. A look, a touch, and his hungry demands ruled her traitorous body. His mouth was teasing every inch of her flesh into response, and her belly tightened with yearning.

Firm male lips took possession of her nipple, his tongue caressing and inflicting pleasurable torment until she arched against him, her hands tightening on his back. He was stretched the length of her, his strong, taut body pressing her down, making her aware of his own aroused need for her. His hand moved between their bodies to touch her soft inner thigh where the flesh was as pale and silky as a rose petal. And then there were no defenses or barriers between them as he possessed her very being, drawing her into a spiraling world of such exquisite sensuality that a cry of abandonment escaped her lips. Their passions fused in an exploding, unearthly flame.

In that one bittersweet moment she realized she had never really escaped him. She would always be a willing prisoner of his arms. She would always love him.

CHAPTER
Eight

SHE AWOKE SLOWLY the next morning in his bed, feeling warm and content next to him. Her lover. Her lips formed the words without speaking them. Her husband. She turned to look at him as he slept. He seemed almost boyish, his dark hair falling onto his forehead, the gray eyes that could turn from ice to fire now closed in sleep. His hand rested gently on her shoulder. The hand that was gentle when he wanted it to be.

Last night he had forced her into telling him at least part of the truth, and then he had seduced her into submission to his lovemaking. One thing he had taught her especially well—it was useless to fight him, He forced her surrender no matter what she did.

But his gentleness had surprised her. His caresses had been soft and languorous, his kisses hypnotic. Everything he did fired a passion she'd never dreamed of.

It was as though the year they'd been separated had only sharpened their desires, making their lovemaking more intense with desperate need. His mouth, his hands,

115

his body—his total being—had demanded that she give up everything to him. And when he had driven her to sweet madness, she had willingly given him all she had to give.

Despite his growing urgency, she'd sensed the gentleness she'd known in him long ago and had feared she would never experience again.

She still couldn't believe she'd understood him right as they lay in each other's arms, just before they'd gone to sleep. He'd pulled her against him and nuzzled his lips against her ear. "Jack still has a job," he had whispered. "I haven't sent him notice yet. I'll tear it up, if you'll promise there will be no more romantic interludes with him, even imaginary ones."

"I promise," she had whispered, and he had kissed her gently.

Now he stirred as she looked at him, and smiled at her. She marveled at the warmth in his gray eyes. They were crinkled at the corners, regarding her with sleepy amusement. "Did you sleep well, *ma petite?*" he asked, and she smiled.

"Quite well," she murmured.

"Good. Then if you're rested, you can be the one to go downstairs and see if Henri has the coffee ready."

He grinned as she feigned anger and picked up her pillow. She threw it at him as she climbed out of bed and heard his laughter as she scurried to the warmth of the bathroom. Humming to herself, she splashed water on her face.

At the office the morning went quickly, and Marla worked hard helping Jack. Brent had sent him to his other office in Quebec City the day before on the pretext of going over some records. Marla didn't tell Jack the trip had been a ruse to make her believe he was fired and on his way to Syracuse.

"I'd say we'll be finished here pretty soon," Jack observed, looking over the papers on his desk.

"Then you'll be going back to Syracuse?" Marla asked quietly.

He nodded and paused. "It'll seem lonely back there without you."

"Thank you, Jack. I've enjoyed working with you too."

"I hope I haven't caused any trouble between you and Brent."

She looked down at her hands. "I owe you an apology, Jack. We've always been good friends, and I'm afraid I led Brent to believe it was more than that. I nearly did you a terrible injustice, and I'm sorry."

But Jack smiled at her. "You could never do me an injustice, Marla. And I wish you only the best."

"You too, Jack," she whispered. "I hope we'll always be friends."

"Listen," he said suddenly, "I think I'm getting hungry. How about some lunch?"

"You go ahead," she said. "I told Brent I'd wait for him today."

When Jack had gone, Marla went to Brent's office to see when he'd be ready. But when she opened the door, she found Sylvia leaning against the desk while Brent worked on a folder. He looked up in distraction when he heard the door and said, "Did you need something, Marla?"

She stared at him, unable to speak for a moment, and when she did her voice came out a soft quaver. "Are you ready for lunch?"

"I'm sorry," he said. "I won't be done for a while. Why don't you go ahead?"

Marla caught Sylvia's taunting look and bit her lip before speaking. She hated to plead with him in front of his mistress. "I'd been looking forward to it, Brent."

"I really wish I could go," he said with a touch of impatience, "but I have to get this work out of the way."

"And it doesn't matter to you if I go without you?"

she challenged him softly.

He looked at her sharply. "I trust you."

Sylvia brushed her hair back with a toss of her head, a gesture obviously meant to dismiss Marla. Hoping she didn't appear as chastened as she felt, Marla raised her head proudly and left the office. One standard for her and another for him, she thought grimly. She looked toward her desk hopefully, wondering if Jack might have come back for something, but he wasn't there. Compressing her mouth, she got her coat to go to lunch. Brent seemed determined to show her who was calling the shots. He used whatever tactics were necessary to extract her promises; then, when he had proved his mastery over her, he turned cold again and paraded Sylvia before her.

Marla clenched her fists at her sides as she strode from the building. She would show him. She could be as calculating as he was.

She wouldn't give in to him. She wouldn't let him know how much he hurt her with his coldhearted treatment. If Brent intended to inflict as much pain as he could, then she would retaliate with all of her stubborn resistance.

A day later Brent informed her casually that Sylvia was giving a New Year's Eve party and they would be attending.

"In a pig's eye," she spat coldly, but Brent only gave her a sardonic smile.

"We'll see," he said.

The night of the party, Marla stubbornly stayed in her room after they left work, determined not to give in to Brent. There had been an undercurrent of tension between them ever since the afternoon she had found Sylvia with him again, and he had been demanding at work, piling several projects on her that she knew he was capable of overseeing himself.

She paced the room, at the end of her rope. She knew he would soon come to demand that she go with him, and she was ready for the battle to come. Let him holler and bully all he wanted. She wasn't going.

When the door between their rooms opened, Marla was sitting at her dressing table brushing her hair, dressed in her nightgown and robe. She continued running the brush through her hair even when he came to stand behind her.

"Why aren't you dressed?" he demanded.

"I'm not going anywhere tonight," she said coldly. "I'm feeling rather tired."

"On New Year's Eve?"

She shrugged. "I don't care what night it is."

"It happens to be the night we're going to a party," he reminded her sharply.

She put down her hairbrush and turned to face him, hoping she appeared as cold and unyielding as he. "I don't have to do everything you want," she replied, meeting his eyes.

"Is that it?" he asked softly, his eyes smoldering. "I thought there must be an explanation for your childish behavior. You're so stubborn and willful that you balk simply because I want you to do something."

"I balk, as you put it, because you're arrogant and demanding, and you treat me like a child."

"No, my dear, there you're wrong. Perhaps my mistake has been that I *haven't* dealt with you like a child. Because right now you're acting like a very spoiled one." His arm snaked out, and he yanked her to her feet. "What you need is a good hard spanking to correct that childish behavior."

"Let go of me," she cried, struggling angrily. "You have no right."

"Ah, but I do," he said in a low, menacing voice. "And maybe if you couldn't sit comfortably for a few days, you'd think twice the next time you were tempted to try this defiant act."

She kicked out at his leg with her bare foot, but her

leg became entangled in her robe and she couldn't connect with any force. Quickly he scooped her up in his arms and dropped her roughly on the bed. She started to sit up angrily, ready to swing at him, but she suddenly found him pulling off her robe. "Let me up," she snapped. "I have no intention of lying here passively while you make love to me. You won't change my mind with that."

"For your information, I have no intention of making love to you," he countered, and she felt herself blushing uncomfortably. "What I intend doing," he continued as he pulled off her robe, despite her squirming and struggling, "is dressing you for the party. Then I'm going to drag you there whether you want to go or not."

He had pulled off her nightgown as well, and she quickly wrapped the bedspread around herself and began moving away from him as he stood up. While he was pulling a dress from her closet, she took the opportunity to crawl off the bed, the bedspread around her, and make a run for the bathroom door.

He spun around just as she ran past him, and he reached out for her. As he caught the edge of the trailing bedspread, she became entangled in it and tripped. With a muffled cry, she fell at his feet, pounding the floor with her fists in frustration as she felt his hands grasp her shoulders.

"Are you all right?" he demanded, and she nodded, not trusting herself to speak. He was kneeling beside her, his hand stroking her hair, and she wondered for a moment why he wasn't upbraiding her for trying to escape him.

But apparently his anger had diminished when he saw her fall. He picked her up, bedspread and all, and this time put her down gently on the bed. Slowly he withdrew his hands from her and looked down at her. "Wear the red dress," he said softly. She opened her mouth to protest, but his wry smile halted her. "And don't think I won't come back up here and give you that spanking if you don't get dressed quickly." He turned and left the room, and Marla pounded the pillow as hard as she could with her fist. Damn him! He'd imposed his will on her again. She was finding it impossible to fight him. He circumvented her at every turn.

Reluctantly she stood and searched for her clothes. As much as she loathed herself for giving in, she had no desire to linger and find out if he would return and carry out his threat.

He seemed amused when he escorted her to the party, and she stared straight ahead, determined to pretend not to notice.

When the maid opened the door of Sylvia's plush Quebec City town house and took their coats, Sylvia herself, resplendent in a silver gown, emerged from a crowd of guests to greet them.

"Why, Marla, how nice you look," she said coolly, eyeing the red evening gown and making Marla feel distinctly uncomfortable. "And Brent, I'm so glad you came." As she talked, she took Brent's arm and led him toward the party, leaving Marla to tag along behind them. Resigning herself to a boring, long evening, Marla let them go on ahead and made her way alone to a corner of the room where the lighting was low and she hoped she could sit in peace, maybe finding someone like Miriam to spend her time with.

But, instead, a young man came up to her as she sat down, and she looked up in surprise to see Marcel. "What are you doing here?" she cried in delight.

"Sylvia's father is on the board of the foundation that gave us the scholarships," he said. "I guess he suggested that she invite us, since we don't have any family here. Jeff has a cold though, and he didn't feel up to it."

"I'm sorry to hear that, but I'm so glad to see you. Here, sit down and tell me how everything's going with you."

Sometime later, she and Marcel were drinking champagne and she was politely laughing over one of his stories when she looked up to find Brent standing over her. "The music's started," he said. "I'm sure young Marcel here will excuse you for a dance."

"Of course," Marcel said. "Nice to see you again, Mr. Stevens."

Marla bristled as Brent tightened his grip on her arm and pulled her toward the other room, which had been set up for dancing. She had to admit to herself that Marcel fancied himself a far better conversationalist than he actually was, and she'd stifled yawns several times already. She should be grateful for Brent's rescue, but she was irritated by his usual high-handed manner. And, besides, Sylvia hadn't let him out of her sight all evening.

In fact, right now she had her eye on them as she came onto the dance floor with her own partner.

Marla and Brent fell into step easily and smoothly, and his firm hand on her waist guided her around the dance floor gracefully. "You've spent the evening hiding in a corner with that boy," he observed, and she felt his hand tighten on her waist.

"If it weren't for Marcel, I would have died of boredom by now," she lied.

"You seem to attract male admirers rather easily. You must enjoy encouraging them."

She felt her face grow warm and snapped, "Some men feel it gallant to keep a woman company when she's alone."

He smiled down at her wryly. "I can't imagine you being alone for any length of time, my dear."

She looked back warily and was about to reply when Sylvia appeared at her elbow. "I hope you don't mind if I cut in, Marla," she said. "Brent is such a divine dancer."

Brent looked down at Marla and asked, "Do you mind?"

She was tempted to say she did, to see what his re-action would be, but instead she murmured coolly, "No, of course not."

She backed away and watched as Sylvia slid into his arms with feline ease. He was still looking at Marla though, and she forced a smile when Marcel came up to her to ask for a dance. He wasn't as polished a dancer as Brent, and he apologized twice for stepping on her feet. But she continued to smile, hoping Brent was watch-ing. When the dance ended, Marcel volunteered to get her a glass of champagne, and Marla found herself turn-ing to find Brent. She searched the group of dancers, and her heart leaped to her throat when she saw him walking away with Sylvia. They were earnestly engaged in what looked like a serious discussion, and Marla watched with a leaden feeling as they made their way toward the door at the far end of the room. As they closed it after them, Marla swallowed hard. Where were they going and what were they discussing that was so important? She sup-pressed a desire to run after them as Marcel returned with the champagne.

She sipped it slowly and tried to focus on what he was telling her, but she couldn't concentrate. Finally she set down the glass and said, "I'm sorry, Marcel. Would you excuse me a moment? There's someone I have to see."

Marla moved toward the door at the far side of the room, irresistibly drawn to it. She made her way through a crowd of people, murmuring her apologies as she went, and then she stood in front of the door. Her mouth was dry as she reached out and quietly turned the knob. She opened the door just a crack, then looked inside. The room was obviously a private one, probably used for informal entertaining. There was a fireplace on the op-posite wall, and Brent and Sylvia stood in front of it, their profiles to the door. They hadn't seen or heard her and continued their discussion.

Marla couldn't hear what they were saying, but as she

watched, Sylvia moved closer to Brent, her upturned face an obvious invitation. Brent put his hands on her shoulders, and Marla couldn't bear to watch any longer. She closed the door softly and hurried back to Marcel.

There were tears of anger in her eyes as she asked him to get her another glass of champagne. She couldn't trust Brent—she'd suspected he was seeing Sylvia and she was right.

When Marcel returned with the champagne, she drank it quickly, making a silent vow to fight Brent tooth and nail from this night on.

Marcel listened to her ask a waiter for another glass of champagne, then commented, "You must have something to celebrate tonight."

"I do," Marla said grimly. "I've just made my New Year's resolution."

She danced with Marcel, stopping to sip champagne often, then accepted dances with several other young men, not even noticing when Brent emerged from the other room with Sylvia. But whenever she caught his eyes on her, he was frowning.

It was almost midnight when he finally made his way across the room to her. The music had stopped, and everyone was counting in unison. Marla was standing with a group of young men she had danced with, and she watched Brent come toward her, his face hard and cold.

The count was down to five seconds when he stood in front of her. "I believe it's customary to kiss at the stroke of midnight," he said, his gray eyes curtained from her so that she couldn't read his expression.

She would have refused, but when the magic hour of midnight was reached and cheers erupted around them, he pulled her to him and brought his mouth down hard on hers. She pushed against his chest, but it was useless, so she stood stonily, stiff in his embrace.

When he raised his head, his eyes were slits of steel,

and she knew he was furious at her lack of response. "Happy New Year," she said contemptuously. "I'm going to get some more champagne." As she started to brush past him, she felt a shudder go through her. He was like granite in his treatment of her, hard and unyielding, but she wasn't going to be cowed by him any longer—no matter what he threatened or did.

"Forget the champagne," he growled in a low voice, catching her arm and holding her immobile. "We're going home."

As he guided her toward the hall closet for their coats, Marla said, "Aren't you going to say good night to your hostess? I'm sure she'll miss you."

Without responding, he gave her a black look and helped her roughly on with her coat. When they were out in the cold air, he pushed her briskly ahead of him to the car, and then they drove home in cold silence.

She went upstairs ahead of him, knowing he'd come to her room and dreading the inevitable confrontation.

She was still dressed in her gown, waiting for him, when the door between their rooms opened and he stepped inside. She stood up and faced him, and they stared at each other across the room.

"I want an explanation for your behavior tonight," he said.

"*My* behavior?" she scoffed. "I might ask the same of you."

"What are you talking about?" he demanded, coming farther into the room and pausing to light a cigarette.

"I'm talking about the fact that you deserted me the minute we got inside that she-wolf's den and spent the entire night with her." She glared at him, seething at the thought of him and Sylvia in that room alone, but determined not to let him know she had seen them.

"Are you jealous, *ma petite?*" he asked sarcastically, drawing on the cigarette.

"No." She fairly spat out the word. "What you do

with Sylvia makes no difference to me. I'm just tired of putting up with this farcical marriage."

He crushed the cigarette out, then closed the distance between them in two quick strides. His arms shot out to grip her shoulders. Recalling the sight of his hands on Sylvia's shoulders, she pulled away from him and tried to run, but he caught her wrist and pulled her roughly back to him. Holding her arms behind her back with one hand, he tilted her chin up with the other. "Look at me," he commanded.

Panting and struggling to escape his grip, she nevertheless lifted her eyes, blue sparks flaring in them.

"We had a real enough marriage one night," he reminded her. "Is that what you want?"

"No," she hissed.

"What *do* you want, Marla?" he asked in a low voice.

She forced herself to stare back at him and answer in an even voice. "I want my freedom."

"A divorce?" he demanded. "Is that it?"

She nodded, and he laughed coldly. "No, Marla. We have an agreement."

"Only until Winter Carnival," she said, deliberately baiting him.

She winced as his hand tightened on her wrists. "You'll have your divorce when I'm good and ready to give you one," he growled. "And don't forget it. You're mine, Marla, until I decide I'm through with you."

As if to remind her further of his possession, he crushed her lips against his, bending her head back until she thought her neck would snap. When he finally lifted his head, she was gasping for breath. "Good night, my dear," he said savagely, flinging her from him. She stumbled backward, then stood with her hand pressed to her bruised lips, her eyes wide as he left the room, slamming the door behind him.

She threw herself on the bed, muffling her face in a pillow so he wouldn't hear her sobs. Was a divorce what she really wanted? She had convinced Brent it was.

And his answer had been to make it clear that she was his property, that she wasn't going to leave him until he was ready to cast her aside. She was only a toy to him, and he was ruthless in his dealings with her.

CHAPTER
Nine

IT WAS MID-JANUARY, and a cold truce had existed between them since New Year's Eve. They spoke formally and politely, and as soon as they arrived home from work, they went to separate rooms to read.

Marla felt cold and lonely, a virtual prisoner.

Henri had already left to begin his retirement, so she and Brent were always alone together in the house. On one such day the phone rang and Marla answered it, since Brent was outside getting some firewood.

When he came in and saw her face he quickly asked, "What is it? What's happened?"

"It's your Aunt Irene," she whispered, her face drained of color. "She's very ill. Her doctor just phoned. He thinks you should come immediately."

Brent clenched his teeth together, but gave no other sign of his concern. "Pack your things," he ordered. "We'll leave right away."

Moving woodenly, she did as he'd ordered, unable to think of anything but the wiry little woman who'd asked her if she loved Brent.

They made the trip as quickly as they could and arrived

at Madame du Bois's home late in the afternoon. The doctor was there, and he took Brent in to see his aunt. When he emerged fifteen minutes later, he appeared drawn and tired and sagged down in a kitchen chair.

"She wants to see you," he said quietly. He lifted his eyes to hers. "Please don't say anything to upset her."

"Of course not," Marla murmured.

She tiptoed into the darkened room and stood a moment to allow her eyes to adjust. Then she moved forward to the bed where the tiny wizened figure was propped up on a pillow. "Madame Irene," she whispered. "I'm here."

"Sit here by me, Marla," the small voice whispered, and her thin hand patted the bed.

Marla sat down gently and took the old woman's hand in hers. "I don't want to tire you out," Marla said.

Irene shook her head, and Marla could see she wanted to say something important. "I like you, Marla," she began, her voice wavering. "And I know Brent loves you."

"Did he tell you that?" Marla asked quickly, her heart leaping.

But Irene shook her head. "He's too proud and stubborn to say the words. I know there's trouble between you two, but he won't tell me what it is. Trust me, Marla. He's a good man, and he loves you."

She started coughing, and Marla, alarmed that Brent's aunt had overexerted herself, quickly reassured her. "Don't worry, Madame Irene," she said. "Everything will be all right with Brent and me. Really."

She hoped Irene believed her, and she tried to look as convincing as possible. "You can make him happy," the old woman whispered, then lay back, her breathing labored.

"I'll get the doctor," Marla whispered, rising fearfully.

Brent went back in with the doctor, and Marla busied

herself cutting some bread and cheese for them, anything to take her mind off the frail woman dying in the next room.

No one was very hungry, and while the doctor gave Irene a shot, Brent sat at the kitchen table with his head in his hands. Marla stood up to rinse her coffee cup, then after a look at Brent, she slipped on her coat and left the house unnoticed. She walked up and down alongside the water in the cold, hunching her shoulders against the wind. She walked until she was exhausted because she didn't know what else to do, but she always kept the house in sight, its small light burning like a candle in the night. In that house were her husband and a frail old woman who'd told Marla that Brent loved her. She knew Madame Irene had believed that, but Marla couldn't. Brent would never love her. There were only lies and pain between them. She continued walking, listening to the sound of the water and no longer feeling the cold.

At least she had put the old woman's mind to rest by telling her that other time that she loved Brent.

Marla walked to the water's edge and stared off at the night sky. There was no point in standing out here avoiding the house and Brent. She would have to go back sooner or later, and she was growing cold. She turned to leave, but a loose rock gave way under her foot, and she cried out as she slid partway down the bank, twisting her ankle. "Brent!" she screamed. She tried to get up, but her throbbing ankle gave way under her, and she fell again. The incline was too steep to drag herself up.

She called his name over and over, knowing he couldn't hear her but unable to stop. Then she lay still. She was growing colder by the minute, but her ankle hurt too much to try to stand again. Her hands and arms were stiff and no help to her. She tried again, then lay back on the cold ground with a groan. "Brent," she cried again. "Brent, I love you."

She didn't even know she'd said it out loud until she

heard her own voice. She had come out here in the cold to escape the truth. Seeing him at the table like that, in such pain, had made her realize the depth of her feeling for him. She loved Brent, but she would never have his love in return. He only wanted revenge for the way she had rejected him; and now, she thought bitterly, his revenge was complete. She was hopelessly in love with him.

She thought she heard a door close in the cold night air, and she cried out his name again. Still there was no sound in the crisp air. She lay back and shivered violently as a great chill washed over her. Her ankle was throbbing, and she was shaking all over.

Then she heard his voice. "Marla," he called, and she answered as loudly as she could. "Brent, over here."

A minute later he appeared at the top of the bank, calling her name. "I'm down here," she cried. "I fell."

He scrambled down to her and quickly picked her up in his arms. Holding her tightly against his chest, he carried her back toward the house. "Are you all right?" he asked anxiously.

"Yes," she stammered through icy lips. "I just twisted my ankle." Dreading his answer, she blurted out, "Your aunt?"

In the moonlight, she saw his profile harden. "She died a few minutes ago," he said hoarsely.

"I'm so sorry," she whispered, and then she began to sob, clutching him around the neck. "I liked her so much, Brent."

"I know," he said quietly.

The doctor checked Marla's ankle and said it wasn't broken but that she should stay off it until the swelling went down. Brent got her some coffee and wrapped her in blankets, and she sat at the table while Brent and the doctor made arrangements. Some men came later to take Irene's body away, and the doctor left with them.

"Let's get some sleep," Brent said wearily. "We could both use it."

He carried her to the bedroom, put her down on the bed, and pulled the covers over her. He took off his shirt and pants, then crawled in next to her, his back to her. She knew they both felt the acute loneliness in the house now, and that was why he was sharing her bed.

Marla lay staring up at the ceiling, thinking about the man next to her. How strange things had suddenly become, now that she'd faced the truth. She wished there were some way she could comfort him. Rolling over to face his back, she tentatively put her arm around his waist. He lay without moving for a moment, then covered her hand with his own.

They were busy the next few days with the funeral and the many details to be taken care of. Marla's ankle got better, and she was able to walk for short periods. Brent was brooding during this time, keeping his grief to himself, but he was kind to her, and each night they slept in each other's arms.

The day they were to leave the island for home they went walking along the bank and came to the spot where Marla had fallen.

Brent stopped and stared out across the water, and Marla stood silently beside him.

When he finally spoke, his voice seemed distant. "My aunt died thinking we have a happy marriage. It was what she wanted more than anything." Marla swallowed, wondering what he was leading up to. If only he would tell her he cared about her, that someday he might come to love her. "You said you wanted a divorce, Marla. For my aunt's sake, won't you at least give this marriage a try?"

"Why?" she whispered, staring into his eyes, willing him to say what she longed to hear.

"Perhaps you'll come to love me someday," he said enigmatically, the familiar mask drawn over his eyes.

She waited in silence a split second, then said quietly, "That would make your revenge complete, wouldn't it?"

His eyes narrowed slightly. "I suppose so. But I thought we could at least try to be civil to each other, for Irene's sake."

"All right," she said in an even voice. "For her sake, I'll give you a semblance of a marriage. No one will suspect we're not a loving couple." She held her breath, waiting to see what he'd say. If he accepted her glib answer that this would be for Irene, then she was safe. He'd never know that she truly did love him, that she wasn't pretending.

He turned to her and put his arms around her waist, drawing her to him. "I'll expect your private surrender as well," he murmured, leaning his head closer to hers until his face blocked out the sky. Her heart was beating wildly, and she clung to his jacket, reveling in the feel of his masculine lips exploring hers. For the first time since their marriage she truly gave in to her feelings and kissed him back with a passion that sprang from overwhelming love.

She longed to have him tenderly hold her and make love to her, and for a moment the need was so overpowering that she moaned against his lips. He dropped his mouth to her neck, and she threw her head back, her hands going up to his hair, twining her fingers in its coarse texture and pulling him tighter against her throat. He kissed his way back up to her face and then pressed her head against his chest. She could feel his heart beating in unison with her own, and she felt she would burst with love.

He held her away from him then, and when her heartbeat had slowed to normal, she slowly opened her eyes to look at him.

"How adept you are at making a man believe your passion is real," he said in a voice devoid of emotion.

She felt as though he had slapped her and she quickly closed her eyes to shield the pain in them from him. When she felt she had her voice under control, she murmured, "I thought you wanted my private surrender. Those were your words, weren't they?"

"How well you play the part," he responded. "But then you've always been good at playacting. A year ago you had me convinced you loved me. It was quite a jolt when I found out it was all a game to you. But now you have to play my game, don't you, Marla?" When she didn't answer, he jerked her head up. "And you're quite a good player. I think I'll enjoy seeing you act the dutiful wife, especially when I know you're pretending."

"Let's go now," she whispered, stung by his cruel portrait of her.

He released her, and they walked back to the house. She thought of Irene's words that Brent loved her, and a bitter grimace twisted her lips.

They had been home in Quebec for a week, and she had fulfilled her part of the bargain to the letter. She fixed dinner for them when she got home from work, and he always made the salad and poured the wine. Together they cleaned up. He had begun regarding her with a new curiosity, and it sometimes made her uneasy, because she was afraid he'd discover her secret.

That particular night, right after helping her clean up the dishes he retired to the living room with a whiskey on the rocks. She sat in the kitchen for a while, sipping coffee and reading, then went in to bid him good night. One glance at the whiskey bottle on the table told her he'd already drunk quite a bit. He was leaning against the mantel staring into the fire, a drink in his hand.

She stood watching him a moment, half afraid to speak. There was a dangerous air about him, as though it would take little to provoke him into violence.

Finally she cleared her throat softly, and he turned to regard her through half-closed eyes. "I thought I'd go on up to bed," she ventured.

He set the glass down on the mantel and crossed the

room slowly. "I must compliment you," he said in a silky voice. "Dinner was delicious. You're playing your part very well."

"What part?" she repeated stupidly.

"My wife. You deserve an award for your performance. Even last night when I came to you, you didn't fight me. In fact, your passion seems to increase each time we make love. If I'm not careful, I might be lulled into a sense of false security. You bait a lovely trap, *ma petite.*"

He pulled her to him roughly and kissed her long and hard. "Pleasant dreams, Marla."

He turned and went back to the fireplace, leaving her standing there stunned. Why was he treating her like this, so cold and angry? She'd done nothing to provoke him, yet he acted as though he were punishing her for something. She didn't understand him. He always hurt her when she least expected it. Unconsciously touching her fingers to her lips, she turned and left the room, leaving him contemplating the fire.

The next day she learned the probable reason for his coldness. She found her stepbrother, Karl, leaning against her desk when she came back from an errand just before lunch. She stopped and stared in blank surprise. "What are you doing here?" she demanded.

"Is that any kind of a welcome?" he asked, running a hand through his hair and giving her a cool smile.

"Considering the circumstances of our last meeting, I think that's all the greeting you deserve."

He shrugged. "Why should you complain? I found you a rich husband—one you were even engaged to. Surely you don't find him totally repulsive."

"You know full well why the engagement was broken before," she hissed in a low voice. "After all, dear Karl, you're the one who opened my eyes to Brent. You arranged to take me to dinner the night Brent dined with Sylvia."

"I considered it a favor at the time," he answered. "Shall I assume that all is not peaches and cream in the love nest now?"

Marla started to reply, then remembered Brent's moodiness of the night before. "Did you talk to Brent yesterday?" she asked suspiciously.

"As a matter of fact, I did."

"And just what did you say?"

"Nothing much."

"You must have said something," she insisted. "I wouldn't put it past you to stir up trouble at any chance you get."

He laughed arrogantly. "Well, there was that small matter of Jack Phillips."

"Jack?" she repeated anxiously. "What do you know about Jack?"

"Well, I did a little checking, sister dear. Don't forget, I know what you told Brent when you broke off the engagement last year. You supposedly left Brent for Jack. I discovered that Jack has been here in Quebec quite a lot recently, allegedly clearing up some of the work you left behind in Syracuse. I suggested to Brent that he might keep a closer eye on you."

"You contemptible pig," she spat at him. If they hadn't been in the office, she would have slapped him, but instead she curled her fingers tightly against her palms. No wonder Brent had been so angry the night before.

"Did you know I rode up here with Jack?" he asked pleasantly, as if they were having a congenial conversation. "I found out he had to come back, so I took the liberty of asking for a ride."

"And what is it you want?" she demanded in a low voice. "You wouldn't come all the way here unless you wanted something."

"Now that you mention it," he said, inspecting his fingernails, "I thought you might be able to solve my immediate cash-flow problem."

"You want money?" she asked incredulously.

"Your husband has plenty to spare. I'm sure he'd give it to you. And then I'd be on my merry way. Incidentally, if you come through for me, I might tell Brent that there never was anything between you and Jack Phillips. Get you off the hook, so to speak."

"You're trying to blackmail me," she said in disbelief.

"Let's just say I have your best interests at heart," he said. "I bet your dear husband doesn't take kindly to the idea that you play the field."

"I wouldn't give you a penny," she hissed. From the corner of her eye she saw Brent emerging from his office with Jack, and she watched as they approached her desk.

Brent's eyes were boring into her. "Phillips has the last of the paperwork to finish," he said without emotion. "I told him you'd help him get it done."

"All right," she said quietly.

Brent returned to his office, and Karl broke the tense silence with a hearty, "Well, what say I take you two to lunch?"

"How generous of you," Marla commented dryly.

Ignoring her sarcasm, Karl turned to Jack. "Come on, Jack. I owe you at least a meal for letting me share your transportation, and I'm sure you don't mind if I bring my stepsister along. After all, I haven't seen her in quite a while."

"If it's all right with you, Marla," Jack said quietly.

"Of course, Jack," she murmured. "I'll get my coat."

Karl took them to one of the nicer hotels with a good restaurant on the main floor, telling them he had a room there. Marla only picked at her salad, feeling acutely uncomfortable with Karl there. Jack was quiet, responding only in short answers when Karl asked him something.

Jack excused himself to go buy a newspaper, obviously ill at ease, and Karl leaned forward to catch

Marla's attention. "I hope you've been considering what I said," he said in a low voice.

"About your demand that I pay you money?" she asked coldly.

"Let's not call it a demand. It's just a request. Or you could call it insurance for your marriage. You know, if Brent divorces you, he could arrange it so that you'd get nothing. He's a very shrewd man."

"I don't care about his money," she hissed.

Karl gave her a calculating stare for a moment, then laughed. "Don't tell me my dear stepsister is in love?"

"It's none of your business," she said. "And I'm not paying you a penny."

"Aren't you forgetting that you told Brent you and Jack were more than just friends?"

"I already told Brent the truth," she retorted.

"But the doubt's still there, Marla," he sneered. "I heard it in his voice when I talked to him yesterday. He seemed very angry. Or didn't he show it at home?"

She glared at him contemptuously, unwilling to have him know just how cruel Brent had been last night. "I repeat, Karl," she said angrily, "not a penny."

Jack reappeared, and Karl changed his smile to one of false warmth. "Here, Jack, let me order you another drink."

"No, thanks, Karl. I think I've had enough."

"All right. Well, if you two will excuse me for a moment, I have to make a phone call from my room. I'll be back down in a few moments. I'm just on the fourth floor, Room 403. You two get yourselves some dessert while I'm gone."

When the elevator doors had closed behind him, Marla turned to Jack and apologized for Karl. "I hope he didn't impose on you for the ride here to Quebec," she said.

Jack shrugged. "It's all right. I guess I just don't let Karl bother me anymore."

"I wish I could say the same," she said ruefully.

They sat together another fifteen minutes, then both grew restless and continually glanced at their watches. After another ten minutes Marla turned to Jack and said, "This is ridiculous. Let's go back to the office without him."

"He did invite us to lunch," Jack reminded her. "We'd be rude to just take off without telling him."

"All right," Marla agreed. "What was his room number?"

"Number 403. We'll tell him we have work to do."

They got off the elevator on the fourth floor and tapped on the door of 403, but there was no answer. "Just like Karl," Marla fumed. "He probably went out the back way and left us with the lunch tab."

Jack laughed. "You're probably right. Karl's not one for picking up the check if he can help it."

They took the elevator back down, and Marla said, "I've heard of elaborate schemes to get out of picking up a check, but this is ridiculous. To say he had a room here."

"He probably went out the fire door wearing one of those rubber noses and false glasses," Jack said, and Marla giggled at the thought.

They were both laughing as the doors opened on the first floor and they stepped out, and then Marla froze in her tracks, the laughter dying in her throat. Leaning against the reservation desk, watching them in cold silence, was Brent.

Marla felt the color drain from her face. She knew what he must think, especially after the seeds of doubt Karl had planted in his mind.

She and Jack walked toward him slowly, and Brent straightened up. When they were standing within three feet of each other, Marla stammered, "Karl had to go to his room...to make a phone call....He never came back down." She searched Brent's face but could read nothing there. "We went to find him."

"Karl doesn't have a room here," Brent said slowly, and Marla felt her legs grow weak.

"But he said—" she began in a quivering voice.

Jack interrupted her quickly. "I don't know what Karl told you," he said, "but it's obvious he was trying to set up Marla and me in some kind of trap. We just had lunch, then went to look for Karl."

Brent gestured toward the coatrack. "Let's just forget it," he said quietly, "and go back to the office."

They walked back without speaking, Marla between Brent and Jack. The wind whipped her hair about, stinging her face, but her mind was on Brent. He still hadn't said anything, and she dreaded the time when he would.

The afternoon seemed to drag on forever. She worked with Jack at her desk, both of them talking in subdued tones. Every time Brent's office door opened, Marla's eyes darted there, but he didn't emerge; just Jean, her face grim. Marla jumped once when her phone rang, but it wasn't Brent summoning her to his office as she'd feared.

About an hour later, she looked up in surprise as Karl sauntered down the aisle past her desk. He stopped to give her a smug smile and say, "You had your chance, kiddo. I just got a call from your loving husband to come to his office. I just bet he's planning on kicking you out of the house, and he's going to pay me handsomely for details of your supposed affairs."

Marla stood up quickly, her eyes burning with fury. She would have hit him, actually did raise her hand, but Jack intervened. "He's not worth it, Marla," he said angrily, releasing her hand. "Karl, go see Mr. Stevens since he told you to come here, and then leave without seeing Marla."

Marla was still shaking when Karl had gone into Brent's office, and she paced beside the desk in agitation until she'd calmed down. "It's all lies," she murmured helplessly. "I never should have started this with Brent.

Now he believes the worst of me. He'll never trust me again—if there's a marriage left after this afternoon."

Tears were gathering in her eyes, and she sank her head onto her hands.

"Why don't you go get a cup of coffee and calm down?" Jack suggested, and Marla nodded woodenly. By the time she got back, Jack told her Karl had already left, looking like a whipped puppy.

"I've just about finished everything here," Jack said solemnly. "Marla, I'll be leaving Quebec tomorrow."

"So soon?" she asked in alarm.

"The rest can be done by telephone," Jack said quietly. "I think it's time we said good-bye."

"I guess you're right," she replied, trying to smile. "I'll miss you, Jack."

"And I'll miss you. Come on now. Let's forget these gloomy good-byes and get this paperwork out of the way."

Jack left for his room shortly after five, and Marla sat down at her desk, staring off into space. She forced herself to do some more work but looked up every few minutes to glance at Brent's closed door. Jean was the last to leave the office, and when she hurried past Marla's desk with her coat, she gave her a sad smile.

Jean's apparent distress only fueled Marla's speculation as to what had gone on in Brent's office and what he was thinking right now. Finally she went to stare out the window at the dark skyline. She didn't hear Brent come up behind her until he lit a cigarette, then she turned to him and watched as the blue smoke curled upward. "Winter days are particularly bleak," he said as if speaking to himself. "The nights even more so."

"They have their beautiful side," she whispered.

"When the snow falls," he allowed. "A blanket of pure snow can make even the sootiest city street look clean."

She found herself growing warm under his penetrating

gaze, and she looked down at her hands. "Brent, about today," she began.

"I know what happened," he said, cutting her short.

She looked up at him quickly. "I still have to explain," she said. He shrugged and she went on, watching the smoke rise from the red ember at the end of his cigarette rather than meet his eyes. "Karl wanted me to give him money," she said. "He said that if I didn't, he'd convince you I was having affairs. He said you'd divorce me and leave me penniless." She said the last in a low voice, feeling she had to tell him everything that Karl had said but not wanting him to think that money was important to her. "He arranged that scene in the hotel when I told him I wouldn't give him any money."

"I know," Brent said in a harsh voice, exhaling smoke. He was staring out the window at the dark, his features tense and iron-hard, and Marla waited for him to continue.

"I'd figured as much by the time I got back to the office," he said. "I called Karl and told him to meet me here. He admitted he was in financial difficulty again and had tried to get money from you." He paused. "I don't think he'll be bothering you again."

"You didn't give him any money, did you?" she cried. "What he tried was blackmail."

Brent laughed harshly. "He got a very fair deal, considering," he said. "I convinced him he should take a job with one of my satellite branches. There's not enough responsibility involved for him to get the company into financial trouble, and just enough salary to keep him out of trouble." Catching her look of disbelief, he added, "Don't worry. He'll have to work for his money. The office supervisor is quite demanding."

"But what if he shows up here again?" she insisted.

"Highly unlikely. The office is in Alaska."

She was silent a moment, then said, "You think of everything, don't you?"

"Some things are unforeseeable," he commented, and she detected a note of emotion in his voice that she hadn't heard before. "Karl's little escapade today opened my eyes to something."

"What?" she breathed.

"When I saw you get off that elevator with Phillips, you were laughing. Then you saw me and a look of sheer terror came over you. I realized you must hate me very much if my presence can frighten you so." She bit her lip and looked away, longing to tell him that the terror was because of what she saw slipping away—any chance of ever having him learn to love her, because he thought she was unfaithful. That was her only fear. But she couldn't tell him that. If she did, she would be stripped defenseless, and he could laugh at her. And if he did that, she would die.

"What I did this afternoon," Brent continued, "was to draw up a financial agreement between us, since a separation seems a very likely possibility, especially since I agreed to allow you that after Winter Carnival. How long a separation it is depends entirely on you." She must have looked astounded, because he laughed coldly. "And don't worry," he added. "You won't be left penniless. The agreement is very generous to you. You may want to look it over after Carnival, before you sign."

She was speechless, her heart sinking. It was only days until the beginning of Carnival, and he fully expected her to leave him after that. Was he bored with her? Was he ready to throw her away for Sylvia? A thousand questions jumbled her thoughts.

He was offering her freedom of a sort, a separation during which she'd be cared for financially. Her heart was crying out to tell him she didn't ever want to leave him, that she loved him. But it was impossible.

She nodded mutely. "Very well," he said. "Let's go home and get some dinner. I've got the papers with me."

He went on talking in a conversational tone as they got their coats, discussing what they would have for dinner, how the weather had grown colder, and how they would spend the upcoming Carnival. But she couldn't concentrate on anything he said. All she could think of was that soon he would be sending her away.

CHAPTER

Ten

CARNIVAL HAD ARRIVED, ten days of revelry in the deepest part of winter, a triumph of light over dark, warmth over cold.

Brent took her out each night for Carnival, and they stood huddled together watching the parades, the canoe and toboggan races, and walking through the city to admire the many elaborate ice sculptures.

One night they stopped at the Chateau Frontenac's outdoor rink to skate and look at the ice sculptures there. Marla hadn't skated since she was a child and spent most of the time wobbling unsteadily as Brent supported her in their tour of the rink. "Time to solo," he informed her.

"But I'm not ready," she protested. Laughing, he released her and skated backward, holding out his hands. "Come on," he called. "Skate to me."

Holding her arms out to the sides to help her balance, she laboriously and clumsily made her way toward him. He called out encouragement all the while, and she was almost in his arms when one foot got out front too far, and she began to lose her balance. "Oh, no," she cried, swinging her arms wildly, but it was too late. Her feet went out from under her, and she slid to her behind right into Brent's legs, sending him down to the ice with her, their arms and legs tangled. They were both laughing, and after a couple of awkward attempts to get back on their feet, they laughed so hard that they ended up sitting back down on the ice. Their eyes met, and they both fell silent. Brent leaned closer, and Marla closed her eyes. His kiss was gentle and tender, and she wished the moment would never end. When he moved back to look at her, she leaned toward him, wanting his warm breath on her face again, wanting him to claim her lips as he'd done so many times before. "We're drawing a crowd," he whispered, grinning, and she looked around him to see two small boys standing nearby, staring. It was obvious from their fascinated expressions that they thought the two skaters sitting on the ice, kissing, were some sort of crazy people.

Marla started laughing all over again. "They probably think we're too old to be doing something like this."

"Give them a few years," Brent said. "They'll be hooked on girls before very long." He helped her to her feet. "You must be freezing," he said, looking at the patches of melted ice on her clothes. "And I bet I know which part's the coldest." He gave a swat to her behind, and she nearly fell down again, leaning against him with a little scream and then smiling.

Brent led her off the rink, and they put their shoes back on. "I have the remedy for winter's chill," he assured her, and bought them two plastic canes.

"What's this?" she asked.

"Caribou," he said, his eyes gleaming with devilry. "Drink up."

She tilted the cane up and took a swallow, then coughed as the liquid hit her throat.

Brent laughed. "I bet you feel warmer already."

"Good heavens," she croaked in a hoarse voice. "You could fuel a jet plane with this."

"A native concoction," he said. "Somehow it makes the weather seem much warmer during Carnival."

They heard someone calling their names and turned around to see Ben and Miriam coming toward them. "A gorgeous Carnival this year, isn't it?" Miriam said cheerily.

"Have you seen that ice sculpture of the outer-space creatures over there?" Marla cried delightedly.

"You sound like you're having a good time," Miriam observed with a smile.

"Wonderful," Marla laughed.

"It's the caribou," Brent confided to Ben in a loud whisper, and they all laughed again.

As they started walking up the street together, Ben and Miriam said they were on their way to a ball. "Brent," Miriam said in a quiet voice, "I was so sorry to hear about your aunt."

"Marla and I appreciated the card and flowers," he said graciously.

"By the way," Miriam said to Marla, "Ben and I are celebrating our thirtieth anniversary in two weeks, and we expect you and Brent to be at the party. The invitations are going out tomorrow."

"That's very nice of you," Marla stammered, suddenly uncomfortable. In two weeks she and Brent would probably be separated.

"We'll expect you then," Miriam said. "And maybe you'll be throwing a party for your first anniversary." She winked and added, "Though if I know newlyweds, that first one is a private celebration."

Marla managed a weak smile as they all came to a stop at a cross street. "We'd better get on to that dance," Ben said, shaking hands with Brent. "You know how women hate missing a grand entrance."

Miriam laughed and gave him a playful poke in the ribs, and they started down the street with a wave. As Brent and Marla stood looking down the street after them, Marla felt as if a spell had been broken.

Brent finally broke the silence as he took her arm and started walking again. "I wonder if we'll be celebrating that first anniversary," he said sardonically, and Marla cringed inwardly but said nothing.

Marla was filing some papers the next day at work when she overheard Jean and another secretary talking.

"It just doesn't make sense to me," the secretary was saying. "Why would anyone buy this company considering the shape it was in? My boyfriend's in accounting here, and he says it was one of the worst investments he ever saw."

"We shouldn't be discussing it," Jean warned in a low whisper.

"You mean because you're Mr. Stevens's secretary?" the girl asked. Jean must have nodded, because the girl continued. "Well, I mean it concerns all of us. If we were that close to bankruptcy, then all the money in the world might not save us."

"Mr. Stevens has a personal interest in this company," Jean said sharply. "He's not going to let it go under."

"You mean because of Mrs. Stevens?" The girl giggled. "So why is the rumor going around that he's divorcing her? She's got to be crazy to let him get away."

"That's none of your business," Jean snapped. "And I'd appreciate it if you wouldn't go around spreading more gossip about any of this."

Marla didn't wait to hear what the girl said. She hurried to her desk, fighting back her hurt and anger. So it was all over the office that Brent was dumping her. No doubt everyone knew about Sylvia as well. Carnival was almost over, and then everyone would know that the marriage was over.

Her anger lasted the rest of the day, and she couldn't stop herself from baiting Brent after dinner when they went to the living room with their brandy.

"I overheard the office grapevine today," she said coolly. "The word is that you bought a company with one foot in the grave and the other on a banana peel."

He regarded her warily. "Your company?"

"My former company," she corrected him tightly. "Yours now. Tell me, why did you buy something that was almost worthless?"

"Maybe it was a better investment than the gossips say," he said without emotion.

A heavy silence fell between them, the crackling of the fire the only sound, until she spoke in a voice barely above a whisper. "Was it worth it, Brent? Was it worth the price you paid to make me live in your house?"

His eyes were burning embers as they watched her. "You'd better watch your tongue tonight, Marla," he said sharply, downing the rest of his brandy.

"Why?" she continued, unable to stop her torrent of fury as she thought of the way he'd bought her and how he was about to throw her away just as easily. "I want to know if the price you paid wasn't too steep. After all, you've only owned the goods for three months, and already you're going to return them. But maybe I wasn't the bargain you thought."

He pushed himself away from the mantel and stalked over to the chair where she was sitting near the fire. There was a strange, ironic smile turning up the corner of his mouth as he said, "I paid a higher price than you'll ever know, my dear."

"I must not have been worth it," she retorted.

"Remember," he said coldly, looming above her, "the separation was your idea."

"But you drew up the papers," she countered in a shaky voice.

"I thought you might come to resign yourself to your

position," he said. His voice sounded oddly strained. "But that seems to be impossible doesn't it? Or have you changed your mind?" When she didn't answer, he said, "Do you still want a divorce, Marla?"

Her eyes locked with his, and she stared into the stony depths, searching for a clue to his real feelings, but she could find none. He hid his thoughts from her without effort, to her total frustration.

If she told him she loved him, would he send her away? No, she thought bitterly. He would keep her with him then, but out of revenge, not love. He would make every waking moment a torture, reminding her daily that she loved him while he felt nothing for her except hate. She would be even more miserable than she was now. No, she couldn't tell him the truth.

"You enjoy reminding me that I married you against my will, don't you?" she said suddenly, surprised at the bitterness in her voice.

He narrowed his eyes. "You haven't answered my question. Do you still want a divorce, Marla?"

"Yes," she hissed. "We have no marriage."

She saw his jaw muscles tighten, and she should have been warned, but still he took her by surprise when suddenly he jerked her from her chair, and her brandy glass crashed to the bricks in front of the fireplace. "We may not have a marriage, my dear wife," he said in a taut voice, "but we still have an agreement." His lips took savage possession of hers, and she struggled and pushed against him.

This wasn't what she wanted. She longed for his kisses, but not like this. He was punishing her with his cruel mouth, grinding her lips brutally against her teeth. His hand caught her hair, and she moaned as he twisted a handful. When she continued to fight him, pounding his chest with her hands, he let go of her hair and pulled her wrists behind her back. Securing them in one hand, he slipped his free hand to her waist and pressed her roughly against the lean length of his body.

He raised his head to look down into her eyes, and she lowered her lashes to hide them from him. He gave a low laugh and began kissing her neck, not gently, but nipping until she was half crazy with the sensations he was arousing in her.

He forced her head up with one hand and surveyed her face again, this time with a triumphant laugh when he read her surrender there.

"As I said," he told her in a low voice, "until I decide to give you a divorce, you'll honor our agreement."

He released her arms suddenly, and she fell backward into the chair, staring up at him, her blue eyes wide with fear.

"I'm going to get some fresh air, *ma petite*," he said in a cold voice. "You may retire when you wish."

She sat rigidly until she heard him get his coat from the hall closet and close the front door behind him. Then she went limp in the chair, gently touching her fingers to her throbbing, swollen lips. She closed her eyes with a shuddering sigh. There was no way out. She dreaded being sent away from him, but she couldn't bear to live with his cruel hatred of her.

She let her tears fall as sobs wracked her slender body. Then, exhausted, she curled up in the chair and fell asleep in front of the fire.

It felt much later when she half woke, but she was too exhausted to force herself to full consciousness. She stirred fitfully and glanced up through sleep-laden lashes to see Brent staring down at her. Her blonde hair trailed across her face like a veil, making her feel that he was part of a dream. She saw his smoldering eyes drop to her lap, and she followed his glance, seeing the pale blue bruise that had appeared on her wrist lying limply there.

Then her eyes closed heavily again. Groggily, she felt him lift her in his arms, cradling her gently to his chest. She murmured contentedly, nestling against him.

It must be a dream, because he seemed to hold her for a long time before he laid her gently on her bed. She felt her dress being slid from her and then the covers were pulled gently to her chin. It must be a dream because his lips were softly brushing her cheek, soothing her with the comforting touch. *Ma petite,"* he whispered quietly against her lips, and she longed to put her arms around his neck, but she felt too heavy to move. She must truly be dreaming, but she wished it would never end.

She awoke the next morning and dazedly threw off her covers to get dressed for work. Pulling on her robe, she realized she was dressed in her slip rather than a nightgown, and in a flash last night's dream came back to her.

She came out of the bathroom, fresh from a shower, her robe pulled around her, and stopped when she saw Brent standing inside her door wearing a deep blue robe.

"I just came to see if you were awake," he said in a flat tone.

"Yes," she murmured, "but I don't remember coming to bed last night."

"You fell asleep downstairs," he said. "I brought you up."

"Thank you," she murmured, avoiding his eyes, wondering if what she remembered had been real or a dream.

"Marla," he said quietly, and she looked at him when she heard the slight command in his voice. "I know all this hasn't been easy on you, but you have strength and spirit." He paused, and she self-consciously clutched at the lapels of her robe, holding them tightly closed. "This is the last day of Winter Carnival," he said. "I told the office we'd close at noon."

"I'll be dressed in a minute," she said. "Then I'll start some coffee."

He nodded and left, and she clenched her hands. The last day of Carnival, the end of her marriage. And he'd come to her room to tell her he admired her spirit. If only he'd said he loved her, this would be the beginning, not the end. But she mustn't think about that. That could never be.

The remembered tenderness of the night before must have belonged to her dream, she thought miserably. Her aching heart had invented the kisses and the whispered words out of a desperate need for consolation.

There was a party at work just before noon. The secretaries had brought cheese and crackers and set up a coffeepot. Everyone was in a mood to celebrate, and they all clustered around the table of goodies in the aisle just outside Brent's office.

Marla watched from her desk as Brent came out to get a cup of coffee and wish everyone well. A whiff of strong perfume caught her attention, and she turned to see Sylvia coming up the aisle in a rabbit-fur coat, her red hair bouncing. She ignored Marla completely and went straight to the table where Brent was standing. Like a moth to a flame, Marla thought angrily.

She couldn't help wondering if Brent had invited Sylvia over to join the festivities or if she had come on her own initiative. The redhead was breathlessly giggling about something, and then she said to Brent, "You can't mean you haven't gone to any of the balls this Carnival, Brent! What's the matter? Has that little wife of yours put a ball and chain on you? Why, you used to be the hit of every ball."

Brent murmured something Marla couldn't hear, and Sylvia laughed again. "Now, I won't take no for an answer," she cried. "I want you to come to my party tonight. After all, it's in your honor."

"Tonight?" Brent seemed hesitant.

"Oh, come on, Brent. You have to come. Please say you'll be there."

Sylvia was leaning breathlessly close to him, and

Marla quickly grabbed her purse and went to the restroom. She couldn't stand to see that brazen redhead sink her hooks into Brent, but she was powerless to do anything about it. Brent apparently enjoyed keeping Sylvia on a string, readily available to him.

When Marla dared come back out of the restroom, she was glad to note that Sylvia was gone, though her heavy perfume lingered in the air. Marla left her purse at her desk, then went to Brent's office to see if he was ready to go home. The office staff had thinned out rapidly, and there were only a couple of people left, both hurriedly gathering up their belongings.

Slowly Marla pushed open the door to the office and saw Brent standing behind his desk, something in his hand. As she watched, she realized it was a small jewelry box, and he was contemplating whatever was inside.

She started to walk inside, and suddenly aware of her presence, he looked up, then snapped the box shut quickly and shoved it into his pocket. Marla compressed her lips tightly and walked toward him. No doubt he was about to present Sylvia with another piece of jewelry. No wonder the party tonight was in his honor.

"Are you ready to go?" she asked briskly.

"Just about," he said. "By the way, we've been invited to a party tonight."

"So I heard," she said coolly. "Though I don't recall my name being mentioned in the invitation."

"Do you expect me to go without you?" he asked sarcastically.

"I wouldn't be surprised," she retorted.

"I accepted for both of us," he said shortly. "You'll be there."

"As you wish," she replied, and she read the surprise in his eyes before he assumed his usual cold expression.

"Good. Now let's go. We can have one more look at the Carnival before it's over."

Bundled in warm coats and scarves, they walked through the streets to pause and admire the ice sculptures again. They stopped once to watch a toboggan race, then went on when it was over and the cheers were dying away. At the Place d'Armes they stopped at the enormous ice castle and decided to walk through. Mostly there were mothers with their children walking there, but Marla spied two lovers laughing together, and she felt an icy pain in her heart.

Made entirely of ice blocks, the castle was spectacularly beautiful. As they approached the entrance, they saw a figure suited up like a plump snowman, complete with red cap and coal-black eyes. *"Bonhomme Carnaval,"* Brent said with a smile. "He's the official host of Winter Carnival." The snowman was greeting the children, and they all stared at him in awe.

Brent and Marla passed by him, and he gave them a friendly wave as they entered the castle. There they stopped and looked around at the wintery palace.

Marla shivered slightly, and Brent put his arm around her. They continued walking, and Marla felt compelled to say, "It's so cold, yet perfect in its beauty. I feel like we're trespassing."

"It's meant to be part of the celebration," Brent said.

"I know. Yet it's so empty inside. It's like—I don't know—like . . ."

"Like a loveless marriage?" he finished for her, and she suddenly paled at his perception.

"I suppose that's it," she murmured faintly.

They walked back out into the streets and headed for their car. Marla was lost in thought and not paying attention to where she was walking when she stepped on an icy patch. Brent reached for her arm as she fell, but he didn't catch her in time, and she ended up flat on her back in the snow.

"Are you all right?" he asked, helping her to her feet.

"Yes, I guess I wasn't watching where I was stepping." He helped her brush the snow from her coat and then took her arm.

"I'd better hang onto you more carefully," he teased

her gently. "You haven't learned to keep your footing on ice."

She smiled, thinking of how they had skated together and ended up in each other's arms.

By the time they reached the car, Marla was shivering uncontrollably, and Brent had his arm around her, trying to warm her up. "We'll be home shortly," he promised her. "You'll get warm there."

He fairly ran her up the walk to the house and pushed her inside. In a few moments he had the fire going and helped her off with her coat. "Stand here in front of it," he commanded. He left the room, returning a few moments later as she rubbed her hands in front of the flames.

"No wonder you're freezing," he commented. "The snow soaked through your skirt. Your legs must be ice-cold. Here, I brought your robe. Take off your clothes and put it on."

She hesitated, and he took over for her, reaching out to unfasten her skirt, then pull it down around her ankles. She stepped out of it, holding onto his shoulder for balance, and he tossed it across the chair. He reached for her pantyhose, but she backed away in embarrassment.

"What's wrong?" he demanded.

"Nothing," she murmured shyly. "I can do it." Under his amused stare, she peeled them off, then shed her blouse and hurriedly pulled on the robe.

"Sit here," he said. "I'll bring you something hot to drink."

He came back with coffee, and she smiled her gratitude as he sat down in the chair beside her with a cup for himself as well.

They both stared into the fire for a long time, and Marla finally said, "Brent, do we have to go to the party tonight?"

"I'm afraid so," he said, but his voice was gentle, not demanding.

She nodded wearily, resigned to it. It seemed they

both felt the change between them now that Carnival was drawing to a close. Fighting over something like the party seemed pointless.

They sat in silence, then went upstairs to get dressed. Marla chose a pale pink dress, much like the one she was married in, with a fitted bodice, full skirt, and lace edging. With her blonde hair brushed to the color of bright gold, she went downstairs to meet Brent. He watched her walk toward him and murmured, "You look lovely tonight."

She smiled, and they left for the party.

Sylvia arched her eyebrows when Marla entered with Brent. "I'm so glad you could come," Sylvia said. "You've been keeping Brent from us. And we've missed him so."

"I'm sure you have," Marla said coolly.

Brent danced with Marla, and they seemed suspended in time, as if the music were playing for them alone. When the music stopped, they stood motionless, his arms still around her, looking into each other's eyes. The spell was broken when Sylvia dashed up to them cheerfully. "I've just got to drag Brent away a moment," she purred. "You'll excuse us, won't you, Marla?"

She nodded stiffly, and Brent followed Sylvia after a quick backward look. Marla made her way to the bar, glancing covertly at Brent and Sylvia, who were making their way across the room.

She got a whiskey and soda and drank it quickly, her eyes burning brightly as she watched Sylvia giggle then lead Brent through the door to the room Marla had seen them enter that time before. Marla clenched her fists at her sides, then ordered another drink in a low voice. She drank that one too fast also, but it gave her courage, and she made her way across the room, her eyes never leaving the door. On the other side were her husband and Sylvia, and Marla was driven to know the worst.

Quietly she opened the door a crack and saw them

across the room in front of the fireplace, just like the last time. As if trapped in a nightmare, Marla could only stand helplessly and watch as Sylvia moved closer to Brent. "Are you sure?" the redhead cried, throwing her arms around him. "We've worked together for so long."

And then Brent lifted her head and kissed her gently on the cheek. Marla couldn't see any more. Tears had filled her eyes, and she pulled swiftly back, closing the door, her heart cold and heavy.

That must be it, she thought dully. Brent was going to send her away and had told Sylvia. Now he and Sylvia could be alone together. The jewelry box Marla had seen him holding in his office would be a reconciliation present for Sylvia. No wonder she had hugged him.

Marla found herself in front of the bar ordering another drink. When she saw the door to the other room opening, she quickly took her drink and made her way to a dark corner and sat down in a leather chair there. She ducked down as far as she could when she saw Brent search the sea of faces for her, then frown. Another man came up to him and began talking, and Marla breathed a sigh of relief. She could avoid him for a little while, anyway. Another drink or two and maybe she could forget the pain that was tearing her insides. But she'd never be able to wipe away the image of Brent kissing Sylvia.

A while later, Brent had moved to the other side of the room to talk to a group of men, and Marla made her way to the bar for another whiskey and soda. She was feeling lightheaded and feverish, but she was thankful for the numbness that was spreading over her, dulling her senses.

She was taking a sip of the drink, ready to move back to her hiding place, when she felt a hand on her shoulder. She turned suddenly, swaying on her feet and spilling a little of the drink. Brent stared down at her with a frown. "How many of those have you had?" he demanded.

"This is number four, or *quatre*, as you taught me in French," she said offhandedly, "but who's counting?"

"I am," he said. "And you're going to make yourself sick."

"I'm already sick," she informed him harshly. "Sick of this party and everything else." She raised her glass in an unsteady mock salute. "Here's to the ending of Winter Carnival," she muttered through her teeth.

"So you're celebrating your freedom," he said icily, his eyes narrowing. "Tomorrow you're going to leave."

"That's it," she smiled brightly. "Tomorrow is the beginning of our separation. After all, you do believe in honoring agreements, don't you?"

His hand reached up as though to touch her face, but he stopped in midair. "But don't push me too far tonight, *ma petite*," he said in a low voice, his jaw hard and tense. "Don't forget that for tonight you're still my wife." He took the whiskey glass from her, giving her a cold smile when he saw that her hand was shaking, and set it on the bar. "You've had enough," he said quietly, then turned and walked away.

"No," she whispered after him so he wouldn't hear. "I'll never have enough to make me forget." She picked up the glass again and went back to her corner.

Sylvia was circulating around the party, and Marla shrank back into the shadows so she wouldn't be seen by the redhead. "This has been the most wonderful Winter Carnival this year," Sylvia said to another woman.

"It certainly seems to have agreed with you," the woman said. "I swear, Sylvia, you look like you're in love. Who's the lucky fellow?"

"Now don't go trying to pry any secrets out of me," Sylvia giggled. "You just wait and see."

Marla ground her teeth in frustration and drained her glass. When she lowered it, she saw Brent coming toward her. Panicked, she tried to rise, not wanting to talk to him again. She could tell he was even angrier by the scowl on his face, his gray eyes holding her rooted to the spot.

But Sylvia intervened. She spied Brent coming that way and stepped into his path. "Brent, my dear, would you have another dance with me?" she cried.

With others watching, he could do nothing but accept graciously. Marla realized she was breathing hard in her nervousness. She made her way back to the bar, one eye on Brent and Sylvia, and got another drink. Now she was really feeling the effects of her hurried drinking, and she sat down on a nearby chair to steady herself. Brent's eyes were on her throughout the dance, and Marla couldn't seem to control her shaking hands.

The dance ended and Brent had just started toward Marla when Sylvia clutched his hand, holding him by her side. "Attention, everyone," she said loudly. "May I have your attention?"

Brent turned back toward Sylvia, softening his expression for the benefit of those who were turning toward them to hear what Sylvia had to say. Marla stood up, her heart beating madly. She didn't want to hear any more. Just seeing Sylvia with Brent made her want to cry.

"I want to propose a toast to my guest of honor," Sylvia cried, taking a drink from a waiter and handing it to Brent. She took one for herself as the room began to quiet down.

Nearly overcome with anger and frustration, Marla hurried blindly for the hall. She fumbled with the coats in the closet until she found hers. From the other room she heard Sylvia calling again for quiet.

Half pulling on her coat, half stumbling, she ran out into the night, nearly falling in her haste. She couldn't get her coat on and started crying in frustration, finally cursing and forcing herself to slow down. Her head was swimming, and in her intoxication her feet could hardly discern the pavement. She finally realized that she had somehow managed to turn one sleeve of her coat practically inside out in her haste and stupor. She made herself take her time, shivering in the cold, and managed to straighten out the coat and get it on.

She started walking down the street, brushing the tears from her face, not really caring where she was going. All she knew was she had to get away from Brent and Sylvia. Her pride would have been destroyed if she had started crying there at the party in front of everyone.

The last of the Carnival revelers were still out. It was dark, and she was having difficulty walking after all she had drunk. It seemed like she had gone a long way when a car pulled to a sudden stop beside her. She stopped and made out Brent through her blurred vision. He had opened the passenger door from the inside and was sitting behind the wheel. "Get in," he ordered, and the tone of his voice left her no choice.

She clambered in clumsily, and her head started spinning again when she was seated. As soon as she had managed to pull the door closed, he pulled quickly away from the curb, and she let out an involuntary groan as everything swam before her eyes.

"I hope you enjoyed your little celebration," he muttered darkly. "If I could have caught up with you when I saw you leaving the party, I think I might have wrung your lovely neck right then and there, I was so furious."

"I hope you didn't leave early on my account," she managed to sputter indignantly.

His jaw muscles tightened dangerously, but he stared straight ahead, his profile uncompromising. Her eyes dropped to his hands on the steering wheel, and when she saw the iron grip, she was glad he hadn't been able to get his hands on her neck.

She leaned back against the seat and wished desperately that she could stop the world from spinning. If only she hadn't drunk so much and so fast. She could still feel the dull ache in her heart and wondered if all the whiskey in the world could ever wash it away.

She wasn't feeling any better when they got home, and she had to lean on Brent as they walked to the house. He hung up their coats, and Marla walked unsteadily to the living room. She stood in front of the fireplace, staring down, trying to focus.

Finally, she felt him come up behind her and she turned, swaying on her feet. "You're drunk," he said coldly, reaching out roughly to steady her.

"How observant," she retorted, flinging back her head to look up at him.

His hands tightened on her arms, and suddenly she found his lips pressed against hers. She twisted her head to escape him, but he tangled his hand in her hair to hold her still.

"Don't," she pleaded as he raised his head to stare down into her face.

"Why not?" His eyes were like chips of ice, she thought in distraction. She mustn't give in to them.

"Because it's over," she said desperately. She couldn't bear to have him touch her like this when she knew she'd have to leave him.

"It's not over yet," he said ominously. "This is the last night of Carnival. You're still my wife, for tonight anyway."

Through her blurring vision she looked up at him in confusion, and then his meaning slowly sank in. "No," she cried hoarsely, pulling away from him. She stumbled toward the stairs, but she was too woozy to outdistance him. He caught her easily from behind, pulling her against him. She tried to pry his hands from her waist, but her efforts were futile. Panting and shuddering, she felt his hands move above her waist, stroking her through her dress.

"No," she cried helplessly. "Please don't."

He turned her around to face him, and she saw that his eyes were unrelenting. "I'm sorry, Marla," he said in a deep voice, already a timbre of passion there, "but you won't deny me this last night."

He picked her up and, though she squirmed and struggled, he held her tightly against his chest and mounted the stairs with her in his arms.

He kicked open his bedroom door and put her down gently on the bed, kissing her until her struggles ceased. She was glad he didn't turn on any lights, because she was sure he'd see the hunger in her eyes and guess her secret. "That's it, *ma petite,*" he muttered savagely. "Just this one last time."

Now she lay trembling on the bed as she watched him undress in the shadows. He came to her then, the pale moonlight outlining his masculine form as he bent over her and began unfastening her dress.

His warm breath fanned her cheek as he leaned close to her. His gray eyes were alight with the flame of his passion. He caressed her neck and face with his lips until she moaned and arched her back, and then he swiftly stripped the dress from her. The rest of her clothes rapidly followed, and then he stood up to let his eyes roam possessively over her slender form.

She was glad the darkness hid her flushed face from him. She was too far gone with passion and intoxication to even try to hide her nakedness from him, and she was unable to take her eyes from his face as his gray eyes swept over her. Slowly he lowered himself to lie beside her and his hands and mouth began an intimate exploration of her hot skin.

His caressing hand ran down the length of her body and she arched her back, bringing herself even closer against him. "Your skin always smells like flowers," he murmured against her ear. "You were made for love."

She gave a desperate cry of passion and anguish, and locked her arms around his neck, whispering his name.

She hungered for him too much to be patient with preliminaries, and she twisted against him as he was greedily feeding himself on the softly rounded flesh of her breast.

"Vixen," he taunted softly, but his breathing was as ragged as her own.

She slid her hand down the length of his leanly muscled body and was rewarded by a clenching of his muscles and a groan of pleasure when she caressed his flat stomach. He dragged her hand to his lips and kissed her palm hungrily, then, unable to prolong the tension anymore, he moved over her and satisfied her aching need. Together they plunged into a swirling vortex where everything was forgotten but their all-consuming passion.

CHAPTER
Eleven

MARLA MURMURED IN her sleep and stretched slowly. She wanted to dream some more, but something was disturbing her sleep, a noise. In her dream she was reliving the morning, when Brent had carried her back to her own bed when he awoke. She had been half asleep, and she'd snuggled against his chest. He'd set her down on the bed and kissed her gently. She could remember that much, but the rest was hazy. She'd been in twilight sleep, and she remembered mumbling, "I have to leave, Brent."

Then, as she was drifting into deeper sleep, she'd heard his voice, but it sounded like he said, "I won't ever let you leave me, Marla. Never."

She must have been dreaming. He wouldn't really have said that. It was only what she'd wanted desperately to hear.

She was trying to remember more clearly what he had said, but something was disturbing her sleep. Suddenly she was awake, looking around in confusion. She was in her own room, and a phone was ringing.

Marla stumbled out of bed and pulled on her robe as she made her way to the hall extension. Her head was pounding, and her mouth felt like it was stuffed with cotton. "All right," she muttered angrily in the direction of the phone. "Hello?"

"This is Pinewood Florists calling," a female voice said. "Is this the Brent Stevens residence?"

"Yes, it is," Marla mumbled, running her hand through her hair.

"Mr. Stevens placed an order this morning for some flowers to be sent, and I'm afraid we've lost the address. I wondered if you could help us."

"I'll try," Marla said, her voice still hoarse. She wasn't sufficiently awake to really understand what this was all about.

"The flowers are to go to a Miss Sylvia Morelle. Mr. Stevens asked that they be sent to her home, and we can't find the address."

Marla stood in stunned silence a moment, hoping she was still dreaming, but the voice at the other end said, "Ma'am?"

"Yes," Marla stammered. She searched her memory for the street number of the town house, then gave it to the woman.

"Thank you," the voice said crisply. "We'll get these out right away."

"All right," Marla said numbly. Slowly she hung up the phone and went back to her room. Brent hadn't wasted any time, she thought bitterly. A kiss for Sylvia last night and flowers today. He was moving Marla right out and Sylvia right in.

She knew she must have dreamed those words last night. *I won't ever let you leave me, Marla. Never.* She wanted so desperately to hear them. She must have invented them from her own wishful dreams and intoxicated state. Sated by his lovemaking, she had wanted still more. She had wanted his love—an unattainable gift.

She sank down on her bed and rubbed her temples. She would have to leave. The only alternative was to forget her pride and stay in the house until he threw her out. And, obviously, he expected her to leave today. Well, she wouldn't disappoint him. She wasn't going to tell him the truth—that she loved him and would give anything if he asked her or even ordered her to stay with him. If he learned the truth, she would have nothing left, not even her pride, which would be stripped from her in the face of his derision.

She would rather have him think she hated him.

She stood up carefully and went to the closet to get her suitcase. Her head throbbed with excruciating pain when she bent down to pick it up, and she gasped. Slowly she straightened up with the suitcase and put it on her bed. She wondered if she should take all the clothes he'd given her. They'd only make her miserable each time she put them on and thought of him.

She put a couple of the dresses in the suitcase. He wouldn't begrudge her those. Besides, they were too small for Sylvia, even as tight as she wore her clothes.

She heard the front door open downstairs and froze automatically. He was back from his jogging. Lately he had taken to getting up early and going out for a run. He said it cleared his mind and helped him put things in perspective. She had thought how wonderful it would be to wake up in the morning in his bed and in his arms and then fix him a cup of coffee and maybe accompany him on his morning run. But it was never to be.

She heard his footsteps on the stairs and quickly composed herself. She would have to convince him that she wanted to leave and that she had no feelings for him whatsoever. She mustn't weaken in the face of his considerable charm, or forceful will—whichever he chose to exercise.

"You're up already." His deep voice came from the doorway, and she looked up, feigning surprise. He was wearing jeans, a blue flannel shirt, and running shoes, and his gray eyes seemed unusually piercing. "I thought you'd still be asleep, considering your condition last night," he said.

"Which condition?" she asked bluntly, watching for his reaction.

But his eyes betrayed nothing. "I thought you might sleep better in your own bed this morning," he said without emotion. Without waiting for her reply, he added, "How do you feel?"

"I have a splitting headache, but other than that I'm fine."

"I take it you're planning on leaving today," he said, walking into the room and gesturing toward the open suitcase.

"I'd really planned on calling a taxi. I thought I'd be out of here before you got back."

She glanced up, and her gaze was arrested by something in his eyes. But whatever it was, it passed, and the familiar emotionless mask was back in place. "Is that all you're taking?" he asked as she pulled the suitcase shut.

She shrugged. "I don't feel I have claim to anything else," she said quietly. "I left the rest of the clothes in the closet."

"And you're going back to your old clothes—your disguise?" he asked.

She turned and stared at him, feeling that he had read her thoughts. "I don't see that it's any concern of yours," she answered coldly.

"You're still my wife," he said, his eyes chips of ice. "Or don't you remember last night?"

"That was the last time," she retorted. "Carnival's over."

"This is only a separation." He gripped her shoulders and swung her around to face him. "Or is it more than that?"

Marla took a deep breath and steeled her resolve. She had to make the break now. She had to be strong and sever herself from him or she was afraid she would break down and ask him to let her stay.

"Brent." She could barely control her voice. "I want a divorce."

She winced as she felt his fingers tighten angrily. "We'll see, Marla."

"No. I want to see the papers you had drawn up. Just send them to me after I'm gone. Or don't even bother. Just have a lawyer get in touch with me. I don't want anything from you, Brent. Just my freedom."

She was quaking so much inside that she wondered if he could feel it in her shoulders. But apparently he didn't, because he appeared angrier than ever. "And where are you planning on going?"

She shrugged, trying to appear casual. "Syracuse, I guess."

"To Jack?" His voice was hard.

"Brent, I told you there was nothing between Jack and me. I'm sorry I lied to you about that once."

"I believe you." She was surprised by his admission but tried not to show it. "Why did you break off our engagement that time? Did you stop loving me?" He paused. "Or did you ever love me at all?"

She made her voice deliberately cold. She knew she sounded heartless, but it was the only way. "I told you, Brent. It was only a fling. I never meant for it to get serious."

"Haven't you ever loved anyone, Marla?" he demanded.

She longed so much to tell him she had never loved anyone until she met him, that she'd never love anyone else, not like this. But instead she hissed, "No, Brent. Never."

"A pity," he said coldly.

"I'm almost ready to leave now, Brent," she said in clipped tones. "Please go so I can get dressed."

"After last night?" he retorted. "No, Marla. If you're leaving, you'll have to get dressed now, while I'm here."

He released her arms and leaned against her bedpost,

watching her through cold, sardonic eyes.

"All right, Brent," she said, trying to maintain her composure. "If you insist." She turned her back to him and slipped on her underwear beneath her robe and nightgown. Quickly peeling off the robe, she finished the job as best she could, then pulled on her slip and nylons. Truimphantly, she turned to him with a cold smile and pulled her white knit dress over her head. "If you don't mind, Brent, I think I'll call a taxi now."

"Don't you have time for a cup of coffee first?" he asked.

She knew she should refuse and leave as quickly as possible, but her mouth was still completely dry. "One cup then," she said, swallowing.

He picked up her suitcase and carried it downstairs, Marla trailing behind him. Her emotions were jumbled, confused. She wanted her last remaining moments with him to last forever, yet she also wanted to get it over with, to get beyond the pain.

He set her suitcase down in the kitchen and went to the cupboard while she poured cold water into the coffeepot.

"I'm sorry," he said, turning to her with an apologetic smile. "It seems we're all out of coffee. I guess I haven't learned to do without Henri yet."

"It's all right," she murmured. "I'll get some at the airport."

"I'll drive you," he said. "We can get some coffee on the way."

She hesitated, then thought about the lonely flight to Syracuse. "All right," she agreed.

"How do you feel? Is your headache any better?"

"Not much," she admitted ruefully.

"I'll bring the aspirin," he said, "and you can take some with your coffee."

She nodded, and he got her coat from the closet and slipped it on her.

As they pulled away from the house, she wanted to

turn and take one last look at the farmhouse so she could think of Brent when she was in Syracuse and visualize him in the house. But she didn't dare look back. He would notice and might guess she was leaving with regret.

He stopped for coffee at a small restaurant near the Place d'Armes. When they were seated, she looked out at the rink and the remnants of Winter Carnival. "The ice sculptures are lovely," she said wistfully.

"But like everything else, they don't last forever, do they?" His eyes were on her.

"No," she stammered. "I guess nothing does."

"I suppose not," he replied cynically.

They drank their coffee silently, and he gave her the aspirin. She swallowed them gratefully, wishing there were some kind of pill to cure her more serious affliction, love.

She was staring into the bottom of her coffee cup when he spoke. "Marla, I think we should set some kind of time limit on this separation."

She looked at him in surprise. "It's not just a separation, Brent. I told you I want a divorce."

"Do you really?" he demanded.

"Yes." She felt a rising panic, though she made her voice as definite as she could.

"I should have asked you last night," he said ruefully. "You seemed content enough to stay in my arms then."

"I was drunk," she said quickly, latching on to the first excuse to explain her complete surrender. Her head was still pounding, and she was finding it difficult to think clearly, especially in the face of his relentless questions.

His hand grasped hers tightly. "Look me in the eye, Marla, and tell me you won't stay here. Tell me you can't give our marriage a chance."

She swallowed hard, trying to control her pounding heart. She moved her lips, but no sound came out.

"Tell me," he ordered. "I'm waiting."

"It's not that easy," she cried, running her free hand across her eyes. "You can't ask me to stay."

"What do you mean?" She had a fleeting picture of him as the inquisitor, determined to make her reveal her secret.

"I have to go," she stammered, standing up and pulling her hand free of his. "I can't stay, Brent."

"Tell me, Marla," he demanded. "Tell me you hate me. I want to hear you say it. I won't let you go until you tell me."

"I can't," she pleaded. Her strength was gone, and she couldn't fight him anymore. If he forced her, she would tell him the truth, and she couldn't face that. She grabbed her purse and ran for the door, hearing his footsteps behind her. She had to escape him, had to run and hide where he wouldn't find her and make her admit her love. She had to salvage her pride. It was all she had left.

She ran down the walk, trying to keep her footing on the snow and ice in her erratic flight. She had no idea where she was going; she only knew she had to escape Brent. She couldn't hold out any longer. If he caught her, she was lost.

Suddenly she found herself face-to-face with the ice castle, and she searched blindly for a door, a place to hide. She pounded against the ice walls, seeking entry, but she could find none. And when she turned, there was Brent right in front of her. There was no place to run.

He pulled her to him. "Tell me," he demanded roughly. "I want to hear you say it."

"I can't," she sobbed.

"Then why are you leaving?" he said, shaking her, and she raised her hands to her throbbing head.

"Because of you and Sylvia," she sobbed. "And the flowers and the jewelry box."

"What?" he asked in a confused voice. He dropped his hands from her shoulders, and she took the opportunity to stumble blindly away from him. She felt him catch the edge of her coat, but she pulled free and ran as fast as she could. She was almost at the street, but she wasn't thinking. She heard him call her name. He was right behind her, and there was an urgent warning in his voice. But she didn't understand. Not until she stepped into the street at a run and suddenly saw the car bearing down on her. She heard the screech of brakes, a horn, and Brent's agonized voice calling her name. But she was powerless to move. Her head was hurting so much that she could hardly see, and his words kept ringing in her ears. "Tell me, tell me," his voice demanded. She screamed, not even recognizing her own voice, and then she felt a tremendous force push her from behind, and she was flung clear of the car's path.

Momentarily stunned, she managed to push herself up from the pavement and look behind her. Her heart stopped as she saw Brent lying in the street.

"Brent!" she screamed, mindless with panic as she ran to him. Pray God he wasn't killed. She didn't feel the throbbing of her head or the bruises she'd sustained when he pushed her out of the way. Her only thought was that he might be gone forever.

"Brent," she cried again, her heart in agony. "My love, don't leave me. Please. Oh, Brent, I love you so."

She knelt down beside him, cradling his head in her arms, kissing his face, which was drained of color except for the bleeding cut on his forehead. She was crying without realizing it, and her tears fell on his cheek. Gently she wiped them away, murmuring his name over and over.

The driver, shaken, called the police and an ambulance while Marla cradled her lover to her.

When faced with Brent's insistence, the doctor let him come home that evening, but only against his better judgment. Marla had paced the hospital corridor until she heard the verdict. Brent would have a splitting headache and be sore for days, but he was essentially unharmed.

The doctor and attendants finally left the house, and Marla gathered her courage to climb the stairs to his room. She slipped quietly inside, feeling almost like a trespasser, and gave a startled gasp as she saw his pale face, the red stain on the bandage around his forehead. He was sleeping, drugged by the painkillers they'd given him. She drew a chair up to his bedside, sat down, and took his hand in hers. This was all her fault, she thought miserably. She should have forsaken her pride and let him laugh at her, rather than see him hurt like this.

Later, she fell asleep by his side, her grip on his hand slackening as she slept. She slumped forward on the bed, her hand next to his chest. She slept that way for a while, awakening later when night had fallen.

The stars were clear and bright, and only a pale glow bathed the room. She looked down at his face and felt her heart stir. He looked so boyish and defenseless. How could she leave him like this? She had to take care of him until he regained his strength.

She stood up slowly and put his hand gently under the covers. She would let him sleep. She could leave when he was all right. She stretched and decided to go downstairs for some coffee. Then, smiling wryly, she remembered that there was no coffee. Well, maybe she could find some tea or hot chocolate. She stood up and started from the room, but something on the wall arrested her attention. Not wanting to disturb his sleep, she didn't turn on a light, but she crept closer to the shadow on the wall, trying to discern what it was.

She stood back in surprise. It was one of her sketches, one she'd done when they were on their honeymoon on the St. Lawrence. What was it doing here in his room? She'd thought they had been lost. They weren't among her luggage when they'd returned, and she hadn't found them in the car. Now they'd turned up on his walls. She looked at the rest of the room, stepping close to the walls to see in the pale light. They were all here, all of them. He'd had them framed and hung here. But why? She couldn't understand it. Why would he want a remembrance of her?

She hadn't been in his room since the night he'd last carried her here, and then it had been dark. The pictures must have been here all along, but she hadn't known it.

She made her way around the room, inspecting each picture, memories of the day on the boat when she'd drawn them returning. It was all so clear. She could remember every minute of their honeymoon. She especially recalled the old woman who'd talked to them in French on the boat. She and Brent had spoken of the land and the old customs that were dying. Because of that conversation, Marla had gotten him the map for Christmas. She looked at the opposite wall and there it was—the map. He'd hung it over his fireplace. She swallowed. It had meant something to him. He'd hung it here with her drawings.

She felt as if she'd entered a secret place and seen something he had never meant her to see. She looked over at his sleeping form and felt an ache deep inside her. Brent was hurt, and it was all her fault.

She made herself a cup of tea downstairs and brought it back to the bedroom, sipping it as she kept watch on the dear face she loved so much. She'd leave after he was better. There was no way she could go now. The doctor had suggested she hire a private nurse until he recovered, but she couldn't do it. She had to stay with him for a while anyway.

She fell asleep that night, her head sinking down onto the bed beside him, her hand curled over his. He began murmuring her name in the night, in his sleep, and she awoke groggily. When she realized what he was saying, she soothed him, whispering that it was all right, she was there. It seemed to quiet him, and she sat silently then, brushing away the hair from his face. On impulse she leaned down and kissed him gently. He seemed to smile in his sleep.

Content, she held his hand and kept a silent vigil during the rest of the night.

She must have fallen asleep near dawn, because the next thing she knew she was awakened by light filtering through the window. She was stiff from sleeping in an uncomfortable position and slowly let go of Brent's hand and stood up, trying to work the stiffness from her muscles. She stood at the window, staring out at the dawn touching the fallow fields, and wondered how long it would take to stop missing the quiet beauty of this place once she was gone.

Brent stirred in his fitful sleep, and she hurried back to his side. "Marla," he whispered.

"I'm here," she said soothingly. "I'm right here, Brent."

"Are you all right?" he demanded anxiously, his voice weak.

"I'm fine," she said in a soft voice. "Get some sleep now."

That seemed to satisfy him, and he slept again.

Marla went downstairs when she was sure he was sleeping again and fixed herself some tea and toast. She sat at the kitchen table remembering the times they'd sat there together eating their meals. It almost seemed like they'd done that forever. It was hard to remember a time when they weren't together. Her life when she wasn't with Brent seemed empty and meaningless. But she would have to resign herself to that again. She would have to learn to live with the hollow feeling and the loneliness. Once Brent was all right again, she'd have to leave. She didn't belong here with a man who didn't love her.

She had been sitting beside him, reading most of that day, when she got up to stretch and look out the window.

A sound behind her caught her attention, and she turned to find Brent's unfathomable gray eyes on her. "How are you feeling?" she whispered from the window, hardly daring to trust her voice. Her heart was thumping against her ribs so hard she thought he might hear it.

"Come here, Marla," he commanded in a soft voice, and she went to the bedside and took his hand.

"Are you all right?" he demanded. "I was afraid you were hurt."

"No, I wasn't," she reassured him. "You pushed me out of the way, but the car hit you. The doctor says it's not serious, but you'll be in pain for a while." She lowered her eyes. "Thank you for saving my life."

His eyes hadn't left her face. "You were leaving me," he stated flatly.

She didn't answer, just looked down at her hands, and he said, "You never answered me, Marla."

"What do you mean?" she asked in confusion.

"I remember the last thing I said. I told you to tell me that you hated me, but you ran away. You wouldn't say it." She stiffened, unable to answer him. "Can you say it now, Marla?"

"Please, Brent. This isn't the time."

"You were saying something before you ran away, something about Sylvia and a box. What was it, Marla?"

"Nothing. It was nothing. It must be the injury that makes you think I said that."

His voice was sharp, though she could detect the effects of the painkiller in it. "I wasn't dreaming. Tell me, Marla."

"I've got to get you something to eat," she protested, starting for the door. "The doctor said you should have some food when you felt like it."

"It's not food I want now." He pushed back the covers and stood up with considerable effort. Marla paled as she watched him.

"Please, Brent. You might hurt yourself. Get back in bed."

He seemed so helpless with the stark white bandage on his forehead as he walked unsteadily toward her. He leaned against the door frame and held onto her shoulders.

"I heard you," he whispered hoarsely. "I was almost unconscious from the pain, but I heard your voice. And I focused on that before I passed out. You said you loved me. I heard you, Marla." His hands tightened on her shoulders, but the touch caused her no pain. "Tell me, Marla. I want you to tell me how you feel. Do you hate me? Do you?"

She could lie to him no longer. She couldn't meet his eyes and not tell him the truth. "Please, Brent," she pleaded. "You'll hurt yourself. Please go back to bed."

"Not until you tell me," he insisted, and she saw that he would risk injuring himself further to get the truth from her.

"All right," she murmured helplessly, all resistance gone. "I was leaving because of Sylvia," she admitted, defeated at last.

"Sylvia?" he repeated. One hand slipped to her wrist and gripped it tightly, demanding a response.

"The florist called this morning," she said, looking down. "She wanted Sylvia's address to send the flowers you ordered."

"You mean," he said with difficulty, staring into her eyes, "you thought Sylvia and I . . ."

She nodded in humiliation, staring at the floor. "Yes, I knew all about it. I followed you and Sylvia at her parties when she took you into that room. I saw you kiss her last night. I told the florist her address this morning so the flowers could be delivered." Her voice broke and she began sobbing. "Last year, when I broke the engagement, it was because of Sylvia. Karl took me to a restaurant. I saw you give her a jewelry box with a ring." She was crying harder now, and his hand gently cupped the back of her bent head. "I knew I would end up like my mother if I married you. Mason, my stepfather, ran around with other women the entire time he was married to my mother. He broke her heart. He gave them presents and took them to dinner and left my mother at home alone. She died of a broken heart." Marla tried to wipe the tears steaking down her cheeks, but Brent raised her chin gently and wiped them away.

"Look in the dresser," he said softly. "The top drawer." She stared at him, uncomprehending, more tears running down her face. "Look, Marla. Please."

She went to the dresser and opened the drawer he indicated. There was the jewelry box she'd seen him holding in his office. "Open it," he commanded.

She did, and there was the emerald and diamond ring she'd seen at a distance the night Karl had taken her to the restaurant where she'd seen Brent and Sylvia. She looked at Brent in confusion.

"It was always yours," he said softly. "Didn't you know that? Sylvia's father is a jeweler. He and my father were good friends. When I wanted an engagement ring for you, I went to him. He set the stones for me. Sylvia brought the ring to the restaurant that night. She gave the box to me, and then I opened it and showed it to her. It was always for you. I started to give it to you several times in the last weeks, but I was afraid you'd turn it down."

"But, Brent," she protested breathlessly, "I saw you kiss Sylvia at her party, before she proposed a toast to you."

"And then you ran away before you heard the rest of the story," he said, mildy rebuking her. "If you'd stayed around, you'd have heard her announce that she's leaving my employment. She had just found out that day that her job application was accepted. I kissed her as a way of saying good-bye after she informed me that she'd accepted the other offer. She made the announcement while you were running away."

"I'm sorry," she stammered helplessly. "That's why you sent her the flowers?"

He nodded, sagging against the door frame.

"But the letter she sent when we got back from our honeymoon," Marla persisted, afraid to believe what she was hearing. "She said you'd sent her flowers and taken her to lunch."

"So you spied on me, you little vixen," he said in mock anger. "Yes, I sent her flowers and took her to lunch, her and the six other women in my secretarial pool at Daricom. "It's a tradition, part of an appreciation day for the employees once a year." Then he smiled at her. "Come here, Marla." He traced a gentle line down her cheek when she stood in front of him. "Sylvia told me once that she wanted to marry me," he admitted, "but after I met you I told her I loved you and I always would. After you married me, I knew she still wasn't willing to let go, so I found her a job in another company, a job so attractive I knew she couldn't turn it down. I could never let you leave me, Marla. I wouldn't have let you get on that plane."

"Then I wasn't dreaming," she whispered softly. She looked into his eyes and saw only love there, and her heart beat wildly. She even felt pity for Sylvia. "You mean you never cared for her?"

He laughed at the thought, and Marla felt the ice melting inside her. The ache was turning into a fierce joy. "Say it, Brent," she whispered. "Please."

"I came to tell you this morning," he said. "Or yesterday. I don't even know what day it is now. And then I saw that you were really leaving me. I love you, Marla. I had to know if you hated me—that's why I tried to make you tell me."

"I couldn't say the words," she whispered, "because it wasn't true." Her heart sang with joy at what he'd told her. "I've always loved you," she murmured. "I would have gladly married you a year ago, but Karl tricked me.

He told me you were seeing Sylvia. He took me to the restaurant when you were having dinner with her, and we walked in just as you showed her the ring."

"Karl," he said angrily. "He's caused us terrible grief and kept us apart. No doubt he wanted us separated last year so he could keep sole control of the company and continue his manipulation of the books. I should have sent him to Siberia instead of Alaska for keeping you from me." Then his features softened as he saw the pain in Marla's eyes. "Give me the ring, darling," he said.

Obediently she handed it to him, and he slipped it onto her finger. "I married you for revenge, my darling. But I soon found myself caught in my own trap, hopelessly in love with you. When you admitted you'd lied about your other lovers, I couldn't believe it. And then I thought you must really hate me to invent a story like that." Holding her hand, he said gently, "Tell me again, my love. I still can't believe it."

"I love you more than words could ever say," she cried, her eyes shining. "Brent, I never thought I could be so happy."

"We were kept apart by Karl's tricks and our own pride," Brent said. "Promise me, Marla, that you'll always tell me the truth."

"I promise," she said softly. Then she saw the pain etched on his face. "Please get back in bed," she urged him. "You're not well yet."

"I'm well enough now that I know I have you," he said, but he let her help him to the bed. "Don't leave me," he said, clinging to her hand.

"Never," she assured him. "How I've prayed that I'd hear you say those words, that you loved me. It was all I lived for."

"And I thought you hated me," he said quietly. "As much as I loved you, I thought you'd be happier without me. You don't know how it tore me up inside to draw up those separation papers."

"I could never be happy without you," she said fiercely. "I drank so much at Sylvia's party to ease the pain I felt thinking you were infatuated with her."

"How could any man have eyes for any woman but you?" he demanded, drawing her head down to his. His kiss was gentle, but still it stirred the fires within her, and her pulse beat erratically knowing that he loved her.

"And now, *ma petite,*" he promised her with mock menace, "I'm going to show you just how much I love you."

"But you're still in pain," she murmured against his lips. "You need to rest, love."

"What I need is you," he whispered huskily. He kissed her deeply, and she felt the fulfillment of everything she had ever yearned for. There was no longer an emptiness inside her. This was what she had missed and run from all her life.

But surrendering to love was not what she had feared. It was not a terrible fate as long as one's lover returned the love in full measure. It was the most wonderful feeling in the world.

"You know," she murmured quietly, her arms going around him, "I was terrified of letting you know I loved you. I thought that would be my final surrender."

"And I was miserable thinking you hated me," he said.

"No more doubts, my love," she soothed him. "The worst is over."

"But if you ever try to leave me again," he teased her, "you know the price."

"A price I'll gladly pay a hundred times over," she laughed, curling into his arms. She could have wept with joy as he showered her with tender, passionate kisses.

QUESTIONNAIRE

1. How many romances do you *read* each month? _____

2. How many of these do you *buy* each month? _____

3. Do you read primarily
   - [ ] novels in romance lines like SECOND CHANCE AT LOVE
   - [ ] historical romances
   - [ ] bestselling contemporary romances
   - [ ] other _____

4. Were the love scenes in this novel (this is book # _____)
   - [ ] too explicit
   - [ ] not explicit enough
   - [ ] tastefully handled

5. On what basis do you make your decision to buy a romance?
   - [ ] friend's recommendation
   - [ ] bookseller's recommendation
   - [ ] art on the front cover
   - [ ] description of the plot on the back cover
   - [ ] author
   - [ ] other _____

6. Where did you buy this book?
   - [ ] chain store (drug, department, etc.)
   - [ ] bookstore
   - [ ] supermarket
   - [ ] other _____

7. Mind telling your age?
   - [ ] under 18
   - [ ] 18 to 30
   - [ ] 31 to 45
   - [ ] over 45

8. How many SECOND CHANCE AT LOVE novels have you read?
   - [ ] this is the first
   - [ ] some (give number, please _____)

9. How do you rate SECOND CHANCE AT LOVE vs. competing lines?
   - [ ] poor
   - [ ] fair
   - [ ] good
   - [ ] excellent

10. Check here if you would like to
    - [ ] receive the SECOND CHANCE AT LOVE Newsletter

. . . .

Fill-in your name and address below:

name:_____

street address:_____

city_____ state_____ zip_____

Please share your other ideas about romances with us on an additional sheet and attach it securely to this questionnaire.

PLEASE RETURN THIS QUESTIONNAIRE TO:
SECOND CHANCE AT LOVE, THE BERKLEY/JOVE PUBLISHING GROUP
200 Madison Avenue, New York, New York 10016